Toward noon, we stumbled on a well-constructed road.

I was confident that it led to one of the principal cities of Kaol. Just as we entered it from one side, a huge flying monster emerged from the jungle on the other side and charged us.

Imagine, if you can, a hornet grown to the size of a bull, and you will have some idea of the winged demon that flew down at me. My sword seemed like a pitiful weapon against the beast's frightful jaws and its large poisoned stinger. I did not have a chance to escape its lightning-like movements or hide from those many eyes that covered three-fourths of its hideous head.

Even ferocious Woola was as helpless as a kitten compared to that frightful thing. But to flee would be useless, so I stood my ground, Woola snarling at my side. My only hope was to die as I had always lived—fighting.

A Background Note about
The Warlord of Mars

The Warlord of Mars is the third in a series of
books featuring soldier and adventurer John
Carter of Virginia. In the earlier books in the
series, (*A Princess of Mars* and *The Gods of Mars*)
Carter is magically transported to the Red Planet,
which its inhabitants call "Barsoom." There,
Carter's fighting skills and gentlemanly ways win
the admiration of many Barsoomians and the
heart of beautiful Dejah Thoris, the Martian
princess who becomes his wife. He also inspires
the hatred of many jealous rivals, who constantly
try to kill or disgrace the gallant Earthling.

At the end of *The Gods of Mars,* lovely Dejah
Thoris is trapped in the terrible Temple of the
Sun, whose doors open only once each year. With
her are two other beautiful women: Thuvia of
Ptarth, a young noblewoman who is John
Carter's devoted friend, and the evil Phaidor,
who is determined to have John Carter as her
own. As *The Warlord of Mars* begins, Carter is
waiting and worrying near the Temple of the
Sun, not knowing if his beloved Dejah Thoris is
dead or alive within.

EDGAR RICE BURROUGHS

THE
WARLORD
OF MARS

Edited by Denton Cairnes
Afterword by Beth Johnson

 THE TOWNSEND LIBRARY

THE WARLORD OF MARS

TP THE TOWNSEND LIBRARY

For more titles in the Townsend Library,
visit our website: **www.townsendpress.com**

Townsend Press, Inc.
439 Kelley Drive
West Berlin, New Jersey 08091

ISBN-13: 978-1-59194-063-0
ISBN-10: 1-59194-063-X

Library of Congress Control Number:
2005936481

Contents

On the River Iss

I was creeping in the shadows of the forest next to the Lost Sea of Korus. I was trailing a shadowy figure who hugged the darker places on the path, so I knew he was up to some kind of evil purpose.

For six long Martian months I had not left the area around the hateful Temple of the Sun. My beautiful princess was trapped inside, far beneath the surface of Mars. I did not know whether she was alive or dead. Had Phaidor's blade found the heart of the one I loved? Only time would reveal the truth.

One entire Martian year—six hundred and eighty-seven Martian days—must come and go before the cell's door would open again. Half of them had passed, but my last view into that cursed prison cell was still vivid. I saw the beautiful face of Phaidor, daughter of Matai Shang, distorted with jealous rage and hatred as she leaped toward my beautiful wife and princess with that long, sharp dagger.

I saw the red girl, Thuvia of Ptarth, jump forward to prevent the hideous deed. But the smoke from the burning Temple of Issus blocked out the tragedy. My ears still rang with the single shriek as the knife fell. Then silence, and when the smoke cleared, the revolving temple had shut off all sight or sound from the chamber where the three beautiful women were imprisoned.

There had been much to occupy my attention since that terrible moment; but never for an instant had the memory faded. All the time that I could spare had been spent close to the grim shaft that held the mother of my boy, Carthoris of Helium.

The race of blacks, known as the First Born, that for ages had worshiped Issus, the false goddess of Mars, had been left in a state of chaos after I exposed her as nothing more than a wicked old woman, and our victorious forces had overwhelmed their army and navy.

Fierce green warriors from the sea bottoms of outer Mars had ridden their wild thoats across the sacred gardens of the Temple of Issus and conquered the First Born. The leader of the green men, Tars Tarkas, Jeddak of Thark, now sat on the throne of Issus and ruled the First Born, while the allies decided the fate of the conquered nation.

I refused the invitation to sit on the ancient throne of the black men. At my suggestion Xodar became Jeddak of the First Born. He had been a dator, or prince—until Issus had degraded him—so his fitness for the high office was not questioned.

With the Valley Dor at peace, the green warriors returned to their desolate sea bottoms, while we of Helium returned to our own country. Here again a throne was offered to me, since no word had been received from Tardos Mors or his son Mors Kajak, the rulers of Helium. Over a year had passed since they set out to explore the northern hemisphere in search of Carthoris, and finally their disheartened people were beginning to accept the vague rumors of their death.

"Let one of their own blood rule you until they return," I said to the assembled nobles of Helium as I laid my hand on the shoulder of Carthoris.

As one, the nobles and the people lifted their voices in a long cheer. Ten thousand swords sprang on high, and the glorious fighting men of ancient Helium hailed Carthoris as the new Jeddak of Helium. His tenure of office was to be for life or until his great-grandfather or grandfather, should return.

After the arrangements were completed, and

my son sat on the throne, I left for the Valley Dor so I would be close to the Temple of the Sun. I planned to wait there until the day that my lost love's prison cell would open. I left Hor Vastus, Kantos Kan, and my other faithful lieutenants with Carthoris so he would have the benefit of their wisdom and bravery. Only Woola, my Martian hound, went with me.

Tonight the faithful beast moved softly behind me. He was as large as a Shetland pony, with hideous head and frightful fangs—indeed an awesome spectacle, as he crept after me on his ten short, muscular legs. To me he was the perfect example of love and loyalty.

The sneaking figure in front of me was Thurid, a dator of the First Born, whose undying hostility I had earned the time I fought and beat him in the courtyard of the Temple of Issus.

Like most of the First Born, he had apparently accepted the new order of things with good grace and had sworn loyalty to Xodar, his new ruler. But I knew that he hated me, and I was sure that, in his heart, he envied and hated Xodar, so I kept watch on his comings and goings. Several times I had observed him leaving the walled city of the First Born after dark. Tonight he moved miles along the edge of the forest and then left the woods and went toward the shore of the Lost Sea of Korus.

The rays of the nearer moon, swinging low across the valley, touched his jewel-incrusted harness with a thousand changing lights and reflected off the glossy ebony of his smooth hide. Twice he turned his head back toward the forest, like some thief running from the law.

I did not dare follow him out there beneath the moonlight. I wanted him to reach his destination unaware that I was following him, so I could see what he was going to do. So I remained hidden until after Thurid disappeared over the edge of a steep bank. Then I ran across the open plain with Woola close behind.

The mysterious Valley Dor was as quiet as a tomb. Behind me was the forest, pruned and trimmed by the grazing of the plant men. In front was the Lost Sea of Korus, while farther on I saw the shimmering ribbon of Iss, the River of Mystery, where it wound out from beneath the Golden Cliffs to empty into Korus. For countless ages, this river had carried the deluded and unhappy Martians of the outer world on their pilgrimage to this false heaven.

There was no longer a Holy Thern up on the balcony in the Golden Cliffs above the Iss. Helium's navy and the hordes of green warriors had cleared the fortresses and the temples of the Therns when their false religion had been swept away from long-suffering Mars. In a few isolated countries they still retained their age-old power, but Matai Shang, their hekkador, Father of Therns, had been driven from his temple. Despite our efforts he had escaped with a few of the faithful, and he was now in hiding.

As I came to the edge of the low cliff overlooking the Lost Sea of Korus, I saw Thurid venturing out on the shimmering water in a small skiff. Several similar boats, each with its long paddle, were resting on the beach. As Thurid passed out of sight around some rocks, I shoved one of the boats into the water, and Woola and I followed.

We went along the edge of the sea toward the mouth of the river. The farther moon lay close to the horizon, casting a dense shadow beneath the cliffs that fringed the water. The nearer moon had set and would not rise again for four hours, so I was guaranteed darkness for quite a while.

On and on went the black warrior. Now he was opposite the mouth of the River Iss gushing out of a cavern in the face of the cliff. Without hesitation he turned into the cave, paddling hard against the strong current. We followed more closely now, for Thurid was so focused on forcing his craft up the river that he had no thought for what might be happening behind him.

It seemed hopeless to follow him into that dark cave where I could not see my hand in front of my face. I was ready to give up when a sudden bend showed a faint glow of light ahead. My quarry was plainly visible again, and in the increasing light from the phosphorescent rock in the roughly arched roof of the cavern, I had no difficulty following him.

It was my first trip on the River Iss, and the things I saw there will live in my memory forever. Terrible as they were, they could not be close to the conditions here before my forces conquered this land. Since we took over, we have stopped the mad pilgrimages down this waterway. The millions who came before had an awful experience. Even now the low islands all along the stream were choked with the skeletons and carcasses of those who had almost completed their journey.

Thurid continued up the river for perhaps a mile and then crossed over to the left bank and pulled his craft up on a low ledge. I did not follow him across the stream. Instead, I stopped close to the opposite wall in the shadow of an overhanging rock. I saw him standing beside his boat, looking up the river, waiting for someone coming from that direction. I soon saw a long boat containing six men approaching.

The white skins, the flowing yellow wigs, and their gorgeous ornaments of gold marked them as Holy Therns. As they drew up beside Thurid, I saw that it was none other than Matai Shang, Father of Therns! The friendliness with which the two men exchanged greetings filled me with wonder, for the Therns and the First Born were hereditary enemies—never before had I known of two meeting other than in combat.

Evidently the reverses that had recently over-taken both peoples had resulted in this unlikely alliance between these two individuals. I now understood why Thurid had been venturing out into the Valley Dor by night.

I wished that I had found a spot closer to the two men so I could hear their conversation, but it was out of the question for me to try to cross the river now. I'm sure they would have given much to have known how close I was and how easily they might have killed me with their supe-rior force. Thurid and Matai Shang eventually got into the long boat, turned out into the river and forged steadily across in my direction.

I backed up and expected to crash against solid rock but soon saw that I was following another subterranean river that emptied into the Iss at the very point where I had hidden. The other boat was now quite close to me. The noise of their paddles drowned out the sound of mine, but in another instant they might see me in the growing light ahead. Swinging toward the right, I hid my boat on the river's rocky side, while Matai Shang and Thurid approached up the cen-ter of the stream.

As they came nearer I heard the voices of Thurid and the Father of Therns as they argued. The black dator was saying, "I tell you, Thern, that I only wish vengeance on John Carter, Prince of Helium. I am leading you into no trap. What could I gain by betraying you to those who have ruined my nation and my house?"

"Let us stop here a moment so I may hear your plans," replied the hekkador, "and then we can proceed with a better understanding of our duties and obligations."

"There are no obligations, Father of Therns," continued the First Born. "Thurid, Dator of Issus, has no price. When the thing has been accomplished, I only ask that you see that I am received at some court that is still loyal to our ancient faith. I cannot return to the Valley Dor or anywhere else within the power of the Prince of Helium."

"It shall be as you wish, Dator," replied Matai Shang, "and I will be even more pleased if you restore my daughter, Phaidor, to me and place within my power Dejah Thoris, Princess of Helium.

"Ah," he continued with a malicious snarl, "the Earth man shall suffer for the indignities he has forced on us. Nothing will be too vile to inflict upon his princess. I wish it were in my power to force him to watch what we do to the red woman."

"You shall have your way with her before another day has passed, Matai Shang," said Thurid.

"I have heard of the Temple of the Sun," replied Matai Shang, "but I never thought that its prisoners could be released before the allotted year of their incarceration. How can you accomplish the impossible?"

"Only Issus knew how, but it was never her way to divulge her secrets. By chance, after her death, I discovered an ancient plan of the temple, and there I found directions for reaching the cells," Thurid replied.

"Let us proceed. I must trust you, yet at the same time you must trust me, for we are six to your one," said Matai Shang.

"I do not fear you, and you need not fear me. Our hatred of the common enemy is enough of a bond to insure our loyalty to each other. And after we have defiled the Princess of Helium, there will be still greater reason to maintain our allegiance—unless I greatly mistake the temper and vengeance of her lord and husband."

Matai Shang nodded in agreement and commanded the paddlers to move the boat upstream. I wanted to rush over and slay the two evil plotters, but I saw the rashness of such an act. It would cut down the only man who could lead the way to the prison holding my Dejah Thoris. If Thurid took Matai Shang to that hallowed spot, then he would also take John Carter, Prince of Helium.

With silent paddle, I swung slowly into the wake of the larger craft.

CHAPTER 2

Under the Mountains

As we went up the river, the faint glow in front of us grew into a bright radiance. The river widened until it looked like a large lake covered by an immense dome, lit up by glowing phosphorescent rock. Here and there, the dome was splashed with the vivid rays of the diamond, sapphire, ruby, and the other countless, nameless jewels of Barsoom that were incrusted in the gold which forms the major portion of these magnificent cliffs. Beyond the illuminated chamber of the lake was darkness—what lay behind the darkness I could not even guess.

They would see me if I followed their boat across the gleaming water, so I was forced to wait in the shadows until they were out of sight at the far end of the lake. I then paddled out in the direction they had taken. After what seemed an eternity, I reached the shadows at the far end of the lake, where I found that the river came out of a low opening. The roof rose again on the other side, but no longer was the way brilliantly illuminated. Instead, only a feeble glow came from small and scattered patches of phosphorescent rock in the walls and roof.

Thurid and the Therns were nowhere to be seen. Here the way was through utter darkness. The stream was narrow—so narrow that in the blackness, I was constantly bumping first one rock wall and then another as the river wound hither and thither along its way.

The stream widened, and I allowed a great, slow moving eddy to take me beneath the cliff's overhanging side and let my tired muscles rest before turning back against the flow. As the lazy current carried me slowly around in a watery circle, my boat twice touched the rocky side of the river in the dark recess beneath the cliff. A third time it struck, gently as before, but the contact resulted in a different sound—the sound of wood scraping on wood.

Instantly I was on the alert, for there should be no wood down in this cavern except what had been brought here by man. My hand shot out across the boat's side, and I felt my fingers gripping the side of another craft. I sat in tense silence, straining my eyes in the darkness, trying to see if the other boat was occupied. I was afraid there might be men on board who were unaware of my presence. The quiet sounds my boat had made might be mistaken for this boat gently scraping against the rocks.

I could not penetrate the darkness, so I listened for the sound of breathing. Except for the noise of the rapids, the soft scraping of the boats, and the lapping of the water at their sides, I could hear nothing.

A rope lay coiled in the bottom of my craft. Very softly I gathered it up, and tying one end to the prow, I stepped gingerly into the boat beside me. In one hand I grasped the rope, in the other my sword. For a full minute I stood motionless but there was no answering sound, and then I quickly explored the craft from stem to stern and found the boat deserted.

Groping along the rocks where the craft was moored, I discovered a narrow ledge that I knew must be the path taken by my enemies. Calling to Woola to follow me, I tied up my boat and stepped out onto the ledge. The great, savage brute, agile as a cat, crept after me. I turned to the right along the ledge, but I had hardly moved when I felt his fangs tugging at my harness. He continued to pull me steadily in the opposite direction and did not stop until I indicated that I would follow him. I had never known him to be in error in a situation like this, so I felt secure as

I moved behind the beast. We went along the narrow ledge through impenetrable darkness. As we advanced, the way led out into a dim light, and I then saw that the trail ran up alongside the river.

For hours we followed the dark and gloomy river farther and farther into the bowels of Mars. From the direction and distance we had traveled, I knew that we must be well beneath the Valley Dor, and possibly beneath the Sea of Omean as well. It could not be much farther now to the Temple of the Sun. Even as my mind framed the thought, Woola halted suddenly in front of a narrow, arched doorway. Quickly he crouched back away from the entrance and turned his eyes toward me as I went by him and entered the room.

It was a fair sized chamber that must have been a guardroom at one time. There were racks for weapons and raised platforms for the sleeping silks and furs of the warriors. Now its only occupants were two of the Therns who had been with Thurid and Matai Shang. The men were talking and were unaware that they had listeners.

One of them was saying, "I tell you I do not trust the black one. There was no need to leave us here to guard the way. Against what or who should we guard this long-forgotten, abysmal path? I say it was a trick to divide us and separate us from our leader.

"He will have Matai Shang leave others else-where on some pretext or other, and then at last he will attack us with his gang and slay us all."

"I believe you," replied the other, "there can never be anything but deadly hatred between Thern and First Born. And what about the ridiculous matter of the light? "Let the light shine with the intensity of three radium units for fifty seconds, and for one minute let it shine with the intensity of one radium unit, and then for twenty-five seconds with nine units.' Those were his very words, and to think that Matai Shang should listen to such foolishness."

"Indeed, it is silly," was the response. "It will become a quick death for us all. He had to give some answer when Matai Shang asked him flatly what he should do when he came to the Temple of the Sun, and so he made up his answer quick-ly from his imagination. I would wager a hekkador's crown that he could not now repeat it himself."

"Let us not stay here any longer," spoke the other. "Maybe if we follow them, we will come in time to rescue Matai Shang and wreak vengeance on the black dator. What do you say?"

"Never in a long life have I disobeyed a sin-gle command of the Father of Therns. I will stay here until I rot if he does not return to command me to go somewhere else."

"You are my superior," the rebellious Thern said. "I cannot do other than what you command, though I still believe that we are foolish to remain."

I, too, thought that they were foolish to remain, for I saw from Woola's actions that my trail led through the room where they stood guard. I had no reason to care for this race of self-deified demons, yet I would have passed them by if it were possible.

It was worth trying anyway, for a fight might delay us or even put an end to my search. Better men than I have gone down before fighters of lower ability than that of the fierce Thern warriors. Signaling Woola to heel, I stepped suddenly into the room. As soon as they saw me their swords flashed from their sides, but I raised my hand in a gesture of restraint.

"I seek Thurid, the black dator," I said. "My quarrel is with him, not with you. Let me pass in peace, for if I am not mistaken he is as much your enemy as mine, and you can have no cause to protect him."

They lowered their swords and the higher ranked Thern spoke, "I do not know who you are, with the white skin of a Thern and the black hair of a red man. If it were only Thurid whose safety was at stake you could go. Tell us who you are, and what mission calls you to this unknown world beneath the Valley Dor, then maybe we will let you pass."

I was surprised that neither of them recognized me—I thought that I was well known by reputation to every Thern on Barsoom. In fact, I was the only white man on Mars whose hair was black and whose eyes were gray, with the exception of my son, Carthoris.

To reveal my identity might be dangerous. Every Thern on Barsoom knew that because of me, they lost their age-old spiritual supremacy. On the other hand, my reputation as a fighting man might get me past these two if their hearts were not strong enough to welcome a battle.

I did not attempt to delude myself with such thoughts, since I knew that on war-like Mars there are few cowards and that every man, whether prince, priest, or peasant, glories in deadly combat. And so I gripped my sword tighter and replied.

"I believe that you will see the wisdom of allowing me to pass," I said. "To die to protect an enemy such as Thurid, Dator of the First Born would gain you nothing. I am John Carter, Prince of Helium."

For a moment that name seemed to paralyze the two men. But it was only a moment, and then the younger man rushed me. He had been standing a little behind his companion and now, before he could engage me, the older man grabbed his harness and pulled him back.

"Hold your ground!" he commanded. "There will be plenty of time to fight if we find it necessary. There are good reasons why every Thern on Barsoom should want to spill your blood, but let us mix wisdom with our hate. The Prince of Helium is on an errand that we ourselves desired to do.

"Let him go and slay the black. When he returns we shall still be here to bar his way to the outer world, and thus we shall have rid ourselves of two enemies, and will not have incurred the displeasure of the Father of Therns."

As he spoke I could not miss the crafty glint in his evil eyes, and while I saw the apparent logic of his reasoning I knew there was some trick afoot. The other Thern turned toward him in surprise, but when the leader whispered a few words into his ear, he drew back and nodded in agreement.

"Proceed, John Carter," he said, "but know that if Thurid does not lay you low, we will be awaiting your return and see that you never pass again into the sunlight of the upper world. Go!"

During our conversation Woola had been growling and bristling close to my side. Occasionally he would look up into my face with a low, pleading whine, as though begging for the word that would send him headlong at the bare throats in front of him.

Several doorways opened off the guardroom. They motioned toward the one on the right and said, "That way leads to Thurid."

When I called Woola to follow me, the beast whined and held back, and then ran quickly to the opening at the left, where he stood emitting his coughing bark, urging me to follow him the right way.

I turned a questioning look toward the Therns.

"The brute is seldom wrong," I said, "and while I do not doubt your superior knowledge, Thern, I think that I will listen to the voice of instinct that is backed by love and loyalty."

As I spoke I smiled grimly.

"As you will," he replied with a shrug. "In the end it shall be all the same."

I turned and followed Woola into the left-hand passage, and though my back was toward my enemies, my ears were on the alert. The passageway was dim, and we had gone only a short distance when we came to two diverging corridors. At the opening to the one on my right, I heard a sound that spoke more plainly to John Carter, fighting man, than could the words of my mother tongue—it was the clank of metal—the metal of a warrior's harness—and it came from close by.

Woola heard it, too, and like a flash he wheeled and stood facing the danger, all his rows of glistening fangs bared by snarling lips. With a gesture I silenced him, and together we moved aside into another corridor a few paces farther on.

We waited and soon saw the shadows of two men on the floor of the main corridor across from our hiding place. They were moving cautiously now—the accidental clank was not repeated. They came opposite us, and I saw that they were the two Therns from the guardroom.

They walked very softly, and each had drawn his sword. They halted close to our hiding place, whispering to each other. "Can it be that we have out distanced them already?" said one.

"Either that or the beast has led him down the wrong trail," replied the other. "The way we took is the shorter way to this point. John Carter would have found it a shortcut to death had he taken it as you suggested."

"Yes," was the response, "no amount of fighting ability would have saved him from the pivoting floor stone. He would have stepped on it, and by now he would be trapped and broken at the bottom of its pit. Curses on that calot that warned him toward the safer way!"

"There will be other dangers ahead of him," spoke the other fellow, "which he may not so easily escape—if he escapes our swords. Consider what chance he will have when he enters the chamber of . . ."

I wish I had listened to the rest of that conversation—I might have been warned of what was ahead—but fate intervened, and just at that very instant I sneezed!

CHAPTER 3

The Temple of the Sun

There was nothing to do now except fight! I did not have any advantage as I leapt into the corridor in front of the two Therns. My sneeze had warned them, and they were ready for me. There were no words spoken—they would have been a waste of breath. Their presence shouted out their treachery. That they were here to attack me was plain, and they, of course, knew I understood their plan.

In an instant I was engaged with both of them, and though I loathe the very name of Thern, I must admit that they are very good swordsmen, and these two were no exception. While it lasted, it was as joyous a conflict as I ever experienced. At least twice I saved myself from a mortal thrust of piercing steel only by the amazing agility of my earthly muscles.

I came near to tasting death that day as the senior guard played a trick on me that I had never seen before. The other Thern was engaging me at the time, and I was forcing him back—touching him here and there with my point until he was bleeding from a dozen wounds, yet I was not able to penetrate his guard and send him to his ancestors.

It was then that the first Thern took a belt off his harness, and as I stepped back to parry a wicked thrust, he lashed one end of it around my left ankle and jerked suddenly, throwing me down on my back.

Then, like leaping panthers, they were on me! They had not considered Woola, though, and before a blade touched me, a roaring embodiment of a thousand demons hurtled over me, and my loyal Martian calot attacked them.

Imagine, if you can, a huge grizzly with ten legs armed with long talons and an enormous froglike mouth splitting his head from ear to ear exposing three rows of sharp, white tusks. Then endow this creature with the agility and ferocity of a half-starved Bengal tiger and the strength of a couple of bulls, and you will have an idea of Woola in action. Before I could call him off, he had crushed one Thern to jelly with a swipe of a paw and had literally torn the other one to ribbons.

The circlet of gold around the brow of one dead man proclaimed him a Holy Thern, while

his companion was a lesser Thern. As I stood for
a moment looking at what Woola had done, I
remembered another occasion when I had mas-
queraded in the wig, gold band, and harness of
Sator Throg, a Holy Thern. I thought it might
prove worthwhile to utilize this Holy Thern's
trappings for the same purpose. A moment later
I was decked out in the yellow wig, gold circlet,
and his harness.

Woola did not approve of the change. He
sniffed and growled, but when I spoke to him
and patted his huge head he seemed to think it
was all right. He soon trotted off along the corridor in the direction we had been going.

We moved cautiously, warned by the frag-
ment of conversation I had overheard. I walked
next to Woola so that we had four eyes looking
for danger. We were lucky we were forewarned.
At the bottom of a flight of narrow steps we came
to a dim chamber. Despite the poor light, we
could see the floor was completely covered by
poisonous snakes.

There was no way we could cross that floor
and felt discouraged. But then it occurred to me
that Thurid and his party of Therns went
through here, so there must be a way. As the
snakes spotted me, they rushed toward us but a
line of radium bulbs inset along the doorway
brought them to a sudden halt. Evidently they
could not cross that line of light.

I began a careful survey of as much of the Chamber of Reptiles as I could see. As my eyes became accustomed to the dim light of its interior, I gradually made out a low gallery at the far end of the room that contained several doorways. I followed this gallery and discovered that it circled the room. Then I looked up and saw an end of the gallery just a foot above my head. I immediately leaped up to it and called Woola after me. There were no reptiles here, and a moment later Woola and I were on our way through to the next corridor.

Minutes later we came into a vast circular chamber of white marble, inlaid with gold in the strange hieroglyphics of the First Born. From its high dome a huge circular column extended to the floor, and I saw that it slowly revolved. I had reached the base of the Temple of the Sun!

Somewhere above me was Dejah Thoris and with her were Phaidor, daughter of Matai Shang, and Thuvia of Ptarth. But how was I to get to them?

Slowly I circled the shaft, examining it carefully. Part way around I found a tiny radium flash torch and saw the insignia of the house of Thurid inset in its metal case.

I am on the right trail, I thought, as I slipped the bauble into the pouch hanging from my harness. Then I continued my search for the entrance. Almost immediately I came to a small panel in the shaft's base. Here was a door that might lead me into the prison, but how was I to open it? No lock was visible. Again and again I went over every square inch of its surface, but the most that I could find was a tiny pinhole.

I looked into the tiny hole, but whether it was only a fraction of an inch deep or passed completely through the door I could not tell. I put my ear next to it and listened, but again my efforts brought no results. I stared at this doorway and its tiny pinhole for an hour. Perhaps something in my pouch might help. If I could find a slender bit of steel, I might fashion a key that would get me into the temple prison.

As I examined the collection of odds and ends that is always found in the pocketpouch of a Martian warrior, my hand picked up Thurid's radium torch. As I was about to lay the thing aside, my eyes glanced down to a few strange characters freshly scratched into the soft gold of the case.

I looked at them, but what I read carried no immediate meaning. There were three sets of characters, one below another:

> 3 R - 50 S
> 1 R - 1 M
> 9 R - 25 S

Then I remembered the Therns talking in the guardroom! The lesser Thern scoffed and quoted

Thurid's words: "And what do you think of the ridiculous matter of the light? 'Let the light shine with the intensity of three radium units for fifty seconds, and for one minute let it shine with the intensity of one radium unit, and then for twenty-five seconds with nine units.'"

The three lines of characters matched the guard's memory of Thurid's words! The formula was written down, but what did it mean? There could be only one answer—the lock's mechanism was opened by light rays! I held the combination in my hand, scratched by the hand of my enemy!

In a gold bracelet around my wrist was my Barsoomian chronometer. This was a delicate instrument that displays the seconds, minutes, and hours of Martian time, presenting them to view beneath a strong crystal just like a watch on Earth.

Timing my operations carefully, I held the torch to the small aperture in the door, regulating the intensity of the light by means of the switch on the side of the case. Would the lock click at the end of those seemingly interminable intervals of time?

Twenty-three! Twenty-four! Twenty-five!

I shut off the light with a snap. I waited—there seemed to have been no effect on the lock's mechanism. Could it be that my theory was wrong?

Hold it! Was that a hallucination, or did the door move? I watched as slowly the solid stone sank noiselessly back into the wall. There was no hallucination here! Back and back it slid for ten feet until it exposed a narrow doorway leading into a dark corridor. The entrance was hardly uncovered when Woola and I jumped through. I watched as the door slipped quietly back into place.

Down the corridor at some distance, I saw the faint reflection of a light, and we headed that way. We discovered a spiral stairway leading up from the center of the circular room.

I knew that we had reached the center of the base of the Temple of the Sun. The spiral runway led upward past the inner walls of the prison cells. Somewhere above me was Dejah Thoris, unless Thurid and Matai Shang had already succeeded in stealing her.

We had just started up the runway when Woola suddenly got excited. He leaped back and forth, snapping at my legs and harness. When I pushed him away and started going up again, he grabbed my sword arm between his jaws and dragged me back. No amount of scolding or cuffing would make him release me, and I was at the mercy of his brute strength unless I wanted to use my dagger on him.

He dragged me back down into the chamber and then across to the side opposite where we had entered. Here was another corridor that ran down a steep incline. Without a moment's hesitation, Woola jerked me along this rocky passage.

After a minute he stopped and released me. He looked into my face as though to ask if I would now follow him voluntarily or if he must still resort to force. I glanced at his teeth marks on my bare arm and decided to do what he wanted. After all, his strange instinct might be more dependable than my faulty human judgment. Off we went, and it was only a short distance from the circular chamber that we came to a bright labyrinth of crystal glass partitioned passages.

At first I thought it was one vast, unbroken chamber, so clear and transparent were the walls of the winding corridors. But after I had nearly brained myself a couple of times by attempting to pass through solid glass walls, I went more carefully. We had gone a few yards along the first corridor into this strange maze when Woola gave out a most frightful roar, at the same time dashing against the clear partition at our left.

The resounding echoes of that fearsome cry were still reverberating through the subterranean chambers when I saw what had caused the faithful beast to make such a noise. Far in the distance, dimly through the many walls of intervening crystal, as in a haze that made them seem unreal and ghostly, I made out the figures of eight people—three females and five men.

At the same instant, evidently startled by Woola's fierce cry, they stopped and looked back at us. Then one of them, a woman, held her arms out toward me, and even at that distance I could see that her lips moved—it was Dejah Thoris, my ever beautiful and ever youthful Princess of Helium.

Thuvia and Phaidor were with her, along with Matai Shang and Thurid. The three lesser Therns also accompanied them. Thurid shook his fist at me, and then two of the Therns took Dejah Thoris and Thuvia roughly by their arms and hurried them on. A moment later they had disappeared into a stone corridor outside the labyrinth of glass.

They say that love is blind, but the love of Dejah Thoris was so strong that she knew me even beneath the Thern disguise I wore and across the misty vista of that crystal maze. Love must be far from blind.

CHAPTER 4

The Secret Tower

I have no stomach to narrate the tedious days that Woola and I spent getting out of that place. We made our way across the labyrinth of glass and then through the dark ways beyond that led beneath the Valley Dor and Golden Cliffs. We finally emerged on the flank of the Otz Mountains just above the Valley of Lost Souls. This area was peopled by the poor unfortunates who dared not continue their pilgrimage to Dor and could not return to the various lands of the outer world where they came from because of the superstitious beliefs.

Here the trail led along the mountains' base, across steep ravines, by the side of appalling precipices, and sometimes out into the valley. We found hostility and plenty of fighting with the members of the various tribes that make up the population of this vale of hopelessness.

But we came, at last, to where the way led up a narrow gorge that grew steeper and more dangerous at every step. Finally we saw a fortress buried beneath the side of an overhanging cliff. Here was the hiding place of Matai Shang, Father of Therns. Here, surrounded by a handful of the faithful, the hekkador of the ancient faith dispensed his spiritual words to the few remaining faithful. Only half a dozen nations on Barsoom still clung to this discredited religion.

Darkness was just falling as we came in sight of the seemingly impregnable walls of this mountain stronghold. To avoid being seen, I drew back behind a large boulder. After dark, I crept out to search for a way inside. Either through carelessness or over-confidence in the supposed inaccessibility of their hiding place, the massive gate stood ajar. Just inside were a handful of guards, laughing and talking.

I saw that none of these guardsmen had been with Thurid and Matai Shang. Relying on my disguise, I walked boldly through the gateway and up to them. The men stopped and looked up at me and Woola, but there was no sign of suspicion. "Kaor!" I said in the Martian greeting, and the warriors arose and saluted me. "I have just found my way here from the Golden Cliffs and seek audience with the hekkador, Matai Shang, Father of Therns. Where may he be found?"

"Follow me," said one of the guards as he led me across the outer courtyard.

Why did I not question how easy it was to enter this place? I guess my mind was so full of that fleeting glimpse of my beloved princess that I had no room for anything else. Anyway, I soon found out I was following this guard into the jaws of death. The main gate had been purposely left open to tempt me, and I, more like a schoolboy than a seasoned warrior, ran headlong into the trap.

At the far side of the outer court was a narrow door. My guide produced a key, opened the way inside and motioned me to enter. "Matai Shang is in the temple court beyond," he said; and as Woola and I passed through, the door slammed shut behind us.

The nasty laugh I heard after the lock clicked was my first warning that all was not as it should be. For a moment I hesitated, all my suspicions now aroused; then, with a shrug, I stepped out into the glare of torches of the inner court.

Up on a broad balcony, thirty feet off the ground, stood Matai Shang, and with him were Thurid and Phaidor, Thuvia, and Dejah Thoris—the last two chained together. A handful of Thern warriors stood just behind the little party. As I entered the enclosure, those on the balcony stared down at me.

An ugly smile distorted the cruel lips of Matai Shang. Thurid hurled a taunt at me and placed a familiar hand on the shoulder of my princess. Like a tigress she turned on him, striking him with the manacles on her wrist.

He would have hit back if Matai Shang had not interfered, and then I realized that the two men were not all that friendly. The Thern was arrogant as he made it plain to the First Born that the Princess of Helium was his personal property. And Thurid's attitude toward the ancient hekkador looked nothing like respect.

When the altercation in the balcony had subsided, Matai Shang turned again to me. "Earth man," he cried, "you have earned an even more horrible death than we can provide for you. But as you suffer your death agonies, know that when you are dead, your widow becomes the wife of Matai Shang, Hekkador of the Holy Therns.

"At the end of one year she will be discarded, according to our law. Dejah Thoris, Princess of Helium, will then become the plaything of your most hated enemy, Thurid, the black dator."

When he stopped speaking, he waited in silence for some outbreak of rage from me—it would have added to the spice of his revenge. But I did not give him that satisfaction.

Instead, I did something that I knew would arouse his anger and increase his hatred for me.

Of all the holy items a Thern venerates and worships, none is more revered than the yellow wig. Next to that comes the circlet of gold and the brilliant jewel that mark the attainment of the Tenth Cycle.

Knowing this, I removed the wig and circlet from my head, tossing them carelessly on the stone floor of the courtyard. Then I wiped my feet on the yellow tresses. As a groan of rage came from the balcony, I kicked the holy circlet and jewel across the floor.

Matai Shang went red with anger, but Thurid only smiled, for to him these things were not holy. I did not want him so pleased, so I shouted: "And I did the same thing with Issus, Goddess of Life Eternal, before I threw her to the mob to be torn to pieces."

That put an end to Thurid's grinning—he had once been high in the favor of Issus.

"Let us have an end to this blaspheming!" he cried, turning to the Father of Therns.

Matai Shang, leaning over the edge of the balcony, yelled, "Let loose the death beasts!" and immediately doors in the base of the tower swung open, and a dozen terrible banths charged into the arena.

This was not the first time that I had faced the ferocious Barsoomian lion, but I had never faced a dozen of them at the same time. Even with Woola's help, I knew I was doomed. For a moment the beasts hesitated, but they soon spotted Woola and me. They advanced with bristling manes and deep-throated roars, lashing out with their powerful tails.

In the brief interval of life that was left me, I shot a parting glance toward Dejah Thoris. Her beautiful face was set in an expression of horror, and as my eyes met hers she extended both arms toward me. She struggled with the guards as she tried to cast herself from the balcony into the pit below. Then, as the banths were about to close in on me, she turned and buried her face in her arms.

Suddenly I saw Thuvia of Ptarth leaning over the edge of the balcony, her eyes bright with excitement. I could not take my eyes off the red girl. I knew that there was some deeper, hidden meaning in her face. For an instant I thought of jumping up onto the balcony, but I could not desert Woola and leave him to die alone beneath the cruel fangs of the hungry banths. That is not the way on Barsoom, and it was never the way of John Carter.

Then the secret of Thuvia's excitement became apparent as she made that purring sound I had heard once before. It was in the Golden Cliffs, and she summoned the fierce banths to her and led them like a flock of meek and harmless sheep.

At the first note of that soothing sound, the banths stopped in their tracks, and every one of the beasts raised his head and sought the origin of the familiar call. They discovered the red girl in the balcony and roared out their greeting.

Guards tried to drag Thuvia away, but before they could act she had commanded the brutes to march back into their dens.

"You need not fear them now, John Carter!" cried Thuvia, before they could silence her. "Those banths will never harm you now!"

There was now nothing to keep me from that balcony, and with a long, running leap I jumped up until my hands found its railing. In an instant, all was confusion. Matai Shang stepped back. Thurid ran forward with his sword. Dejah Thoris wielded her heavy irons and struck everyone around her! I don't know how she missed Thuvia. Matai Shang managed to grab her around the waist and dragged her through a door. Thurid hesitated for a moment, and then, fearing that the Father of Therns would escape him with the prize, he, too, dashed from the balcony.

Phaidor stayed and ordered two of the guards to carry Thuvia out and the other guards to stop me from following. Then she cried out toward me, "John Carter! For the last time I offer you the love of Phaidor, daughter of the Holy Hekkador. Accept me and your princess will be returned to the court of her grandfather. You shall live in peace and happiness. Refuse me, and the fate that my father has threatened will fall on Dejah Thoris!

"You cannot save her now, for by this time they have reached a place where even you can not follow. Refuse, and nothing can save you! The way into this stronghold of the Holy Therns was made easy for you, but the way forward has been made impossible! What do you say?"

"You knew my answer, Phaidor, before you even spoke!"

"Make way for John Carter, Prince of Helium!" I shouted at the guards as I leaped over the low railing and drew my sword. There were three of them, but Phaidor must have guessed the outcome of this fight. She turned and fled from the balcony.

The three guardsmen rushed me at the same time, and that gave me an advantage as they bumped into one another on the narrow balcony. The front man actually stumbled onto my blade. I jerked it free, and then my blade flew through the air with a swiftness and accuracy that threw the two remaining Therns into despair.

When at last my sharp steel found the heart of one of them, the other turned to flee. Guessing that his steps would lead where I wanted to follow, I let him keep far enough ahead to think that he was safely escaping. He raced through several inner chambers until he dashed up a spiral runway. At the upper end, we came out into a small chamber with a single window overlooking the slopes of Otz and the Valley of Lost Souls beyond.

Here the fellow tore frantically at what appeared to be a blank wall. I guessed that it was a secret exit from the room, so I paused to let him open it. I did not want to take the life of this poor fool—all I wanted was a clear road in pursuit of Dejah Thoris, my long-lost princess.

But, try as he would, the panel would not yield, and eventually he gave up and turned to face me. "Go on your way, Thern," I said to him, pointing toward the entrance. "I have no quarrel with you, nor do I want your life. Go!"

For answer, he attacked me so suddenly that I almost went down. So there was nothing else to do but to give him what he desired. I did not want to be delayed in this chamber while Matai Shang and Thurid made off with Dejah Thoris and Thuvia.

The fellow was a clever swordsman—resourceful and extremely tricky. In fact, he seemed never to have heard that there existed such a thing as a code of honor. He repeatedly violated a dozen Barsoomian fighting customs that an honorable man would rather die than ignore. He even went so far as to snatch his holy wig from his head and throw it in my face to blind me.

When he made his thrust, however, I was not there, for I had fought with Therns before. While none had ever resorted to precisely that same trick, I knew them to be the least honorable and most treacherous fighters on Mars. I was always on the alert for some new tactic when I was engaged with one of their race.

Finally he drew his dagger and hurled it at me at the same instant he rushed me with his sword. A single sweep of my own blade caught the flying weapon, and it clattered against the far wall. Then, as I sidestepped my antagonist's rush, I let him have my point full in the stomach as he went by. My weapon passed clear through his body, and with a frightful shriek he sank to the floor, dead.

Halting only for an instant to wrench my sword from his carcass, I ran across the chamber to the blank wall and sought for the secret of its lock. I tried to force the thing, but the cold, unyielding stone did not budge. In disgust, I stepped to the chamber's single window.

The slopes of Otz and the distant Valley of Lost Souls held nothing of interest but, towering far above me, the tower's carved wall caught my attention. Somewhere within that massive pile was Dejah Thoris. Above me I could see windows. Up there, climbing up that wall, was the only way I could reach her. The risk was great, but not too great when the fate of a wonderful woman was at stake.

I glanced below to where the base of the wall met the jagged granite boulders at the brink of a frightful gorge. Down there was death if my fingers lost their hold for a fraction of a second. But there was no other way and, with a shudder, I stepped to the window's outer sill and began my perilous ascent.

Fifty feet above me was a series of projecting cylindrical stones some six inches in diameter. These apparently circled the tower at six-foot intervals, in bands six feet apart. Each stone cylinder protruded some four or five inches beyond the surface. They looked like an easy mode of ascent could I only reach them.

I climbed toward them by way of some windows. I hoped that I might find an entry into the tower through one of these and find an easier path to continue my search. I reached a point where my fingers could just clutch the sill of a window, and I was on the point of breathing a sigh of relief when I heard the sound of voices.

"He will never be able to solve the secret of that lock." The voice was Matai Shang's. "Let us go to the hangar and take off, so we will be far to the south before he finds another way."

"All things seem possible to that vile calot," replied Thurid's voice.

"Then let us go quickly," said Matai Shang. "But to be doubly sure, I will leave two warriors to patrol this runway. Later they may follow us on another flier—overtaking us at Kaol."

My fingers never reached the window's sill. At the first sound of the voices, I drew back my hand and waited, flattened against the wall, hardly daring to breathe. What a horrible place to be discovered by Thurid! He only had to lean out the window and push me with his sword's point into eternity.

The sound of the voices became fainter, and once again I started my ascent, now more difficult since I must avoid the windows. Matai Shang's reference to the hangar and the fliers indicated that my destination was the roof of the tower, and I set off toward this distant goal.

Some ten feet below the roof, the wall inclined slightly inward, and the climbing was easier, so that my fingers soon clutched the edge at the top of the tower. As I looked over the edge, I saw a flier all ready to rise. On her deck were Matai Shang, Phaidor, Dejah Thoris, Thuvia, and a few Thern warriors. Thurid was in the act of getting on board.

He was facing away, not ten paces from me,

and I could not guess what cruel freak of fate made him turn around just at that moment. But turn he did; and when his eyes met mine his wicked face lit up with a malignant smile as he leaped toward me while I was trying to scramble up onto the roof.

Dejah Thoris must have seen me at the same instant, for she screamed a useless warning just as Thurid's foot landed full in my face. Like a felled ox, I tumbled backward over the tower's side.

CHAPTER
5

On the Kaolian Road

If there is a fate that is sometimes cruel to me, there is also a kind and merciful Providence which occasionally watches over me. As I toppled from the tower into the horrid abyss below, I considered myself already dead. Thurid must have thought the same, for he did not even trouble to look as he turned and mounted the waiting flier.

I only fell ten feet, and then a loop of my tough, leather harness caught on one of the stone projections in the tower's surface—and held. I could not believe the miracle that saved me from death, and for a moment I hung there, cold sweat coming out of every pore of my body.

I worked myself back to a firm position but hesitated to go back up, since I did not know if Thurid was still waiting for me. Soon I heard the sound of a flier taking off, and as the sound grew fainter, I realized that the party had left for the

North. I cautiously retraced my way to the roof and raised my eyes once more above its edge. To my relief, there was no one in sight, and a moment later I stood safely on its surface.

It only took an instant to run to the hangar and drag out another flier. I then flew down to the inner court where I had last seen Woola, and to my immense relief found the faithful beast patiently waiting for me. The twelve banths were in the doorways of their lairs, eyeing him and growling ominously, but they had not disobeyed Thuvia's command. I thanked the fate that had made her their trainer inside the Golden Cliffs. Woola leaped in joy as the flier touched the pavement! He then bounded to the deck beside me, and I tried to take off. In his frantic happiness, he almost caused me to wreck the aircraft.

Despite the shouting of Thern guardsmen, we climbed high above the last fortress of the Holy Therns and then raced straight toward the North and Kaol, the destination that I heard from Matai Shang. Far ahead, just a tiny speck in the distance, I spotted another flier. It had to be the one that carried my lost love and my enemies.

I had gained on the craft by nightfall, and then, knowing that they must have seen me and would not show their lights after dark, I set my destination compass on her. This was a wonderful Martian tracking device, that once tuned in on an object of interest, points toward that object no matter how it might change its location. All that night we raced through the Barsoomian void, passing over low hills and dead sea bottoms, above long-deserted cities and populous centers of red Martian habitation.

The dawning of the day showed that I had gained appreciably on the flier. It was a larger craft than mine and not so swift; but even so, we had covered an immense distance since the flight began. The change in vegetation below showed me that we were rapidly nearing the equator. I was now near enough to the other ship to use my bow gun, but I was afraid to shoot at the craft that carried my princess.

Thurid was deterred by no such scruples. It must have been difficult for him to believe that it was John Carter who followed them, but he could not doubt his own eyes. He trained their stern gun at me, and a shell whizzed close above my deck.

The black's next shot was more accurate, striking my flier on the prow and exploding on contact, ripping the bow buoyancy tanks wide open and disabling the engine. My bow dropped so quickly that I barely had time to lash Woola to the deck and buckle my own harness to a rail before the craft was hanging stern up and making her last long drop to ground.

Her stern buoyancy tanks prevented her from

dropping like a rock but Thurid was now aiming at these vulnerable areas. He wanted me dead from the swift fall that would follow a successful shot. Thurid continued to shoot at us on our way down, but by a miracle, neither Woola nor I was hit. This good fortune could not last for long, and I knew that Thurid would not want to leave me alive again. I waited for the next shell that hit and threw my hands above my head and crumpled, limp and inert, hanging in my harness like a corpse.

The ruse worked, and Thurid stopped firing. I heard the sound of whirring propellers going off into the distance and realized that I was safe. Slowly, the stricken flier sank to the ground, and when I freed myself and Woola from the wreckage, I found that we were on the edge of a natural forest. This was a rare thing on the dying planet of Mars.

From books and travelers I had learned something of the little known land of Kaol, which lies along the equator almost halfway around the planet from Helium. It comprises a sunken area of extreme tropical heat and is inhabited by a nation of red men varying little in manners, customs, and appearance from the other red men of Barsoom.

I knew that they were among those of the outer world who still clung to the discredited religion of the Holy Therns, and that Matai Shang would find a safe refuge here. And I knew that John Carter could look for nothing better than death at their hands.

The isolation of the Kaolians is caused by the fact that no waterway connects their land with that of any other nation. They have no need of a waterway, since the low, swampy land that makes up the entire area of their domain supplies plenty of water for their abundant tropical crops.

For great distances in all directions, rugged hills and arid stretches of dead sea bottom discourage any interface with these people. Since there is practically no such thing as foreign commerce on warlike Barsoom, where each nation is sufficient to itself, little has been known about the court of the Jeddak of Kaol and his numerous strange, but interesting, people. Occasional hunting parties have traveled to this out-of-the-way corner of the globe, but the hostility of the natives has usually brought disaster.

I knew I was on the verge of the land of the Kaols, but I had no idea in what direction to search for Dejah Thoris, or how far into the heart of the forest I might have to go.

But this was not true for Woola! I had barely untangled him when he raised his head in the air and started sniffing and circling around at the edge of the forest. After a while he stopped and,

turning to see if I was following, set off straight
into the maze of trees in the direction we had
been going before Thurid's shot had put an end
to our flier. I stumbled after him down a steep
slope beginning at the forest's edge.

Immense trees reared their heads far above
us, their foliage shutting off the slightest glimpse
of the sky. It was easy to see why the Kaolians
needed no navy; their cities, hidden in the midst
of this towering forest, must be entirely invisible
from above. Only the smallest fliers could
attempt to land here.

I learned later that slender watchtowers rise
to the top level of the forest in each city of Kaol.
These towers guard the Kaolians against any
secret approach of a hostile fleet. The hekkador
of the Holy Therns landed at one of the towers,
and his party was safely lowered to the ground.

As Woola and I approached the bottom of
the slope, the ground became mushy, so it was
difficult to make any headway whatever. Slender
purple grasses topped with red and yellow fern-
like fronds grew to a height several feet above my
head. Creeping vines hung in graceful loops from
tree to tree, and among them were several varieties of the Martian "man-flower," whose
blooms have eyes and hands and seize the small
animals that make up their diet.

I also saw a few of the repulsive calot trees. It

is a carnivorous plant about the size of the sage-
brush that dots our western plains. Each branch
ends in a set of strong jaws, which drag down and
devour large and formidable beasts of prey. Both
Woola and I had several narrow escapes from
these greedy, woodland monsters.

Occasional areas of firm sod gave us intervals
of rest from the labor of traveling across this gorgeous swamp, and it was on one of these that I
finally decided to make camp for I knew that
nightfall was fast approaching.

Many varieties of fruit grew in abundance
around us, and as Martian calots are omnivorous,
Woola and I had no difficulty in making a meal.
Afterward, I lay down with my back to my faithful hound and dropped into a deep and dreamless
sleep.

The forest was shrouded in impenetrable
darkness when a low growl from Woola awak-
ened me. All around us I heard the quiet movement of large, padded feet and now and then the
wicked gleam of green eyes. I got up, drew my
sword, and waited.

Suddenly a loud, horrid roar burst from some
savage throat that seemed to be standing right
next to me! I was foolish not to have climbed up
the branches of one of the countless trees that
surrounded us! By daylight it would have been
comparatively easy to go up and make a sleeping

platform, but now it was too late. There was nothing else to do but to stand our ground.

From the hideous racket all around us, I judged that we were in the midst of hundreds of the fierce, man-eating creatures of the Kaolian jungle. They kept up their infernal din for the rest of the night, but why they did not attack us, I could not guess, nor am I sure to this day, unless it is that none of them ever venture on the patches of flat meadowland which dot the swamp.

When morning broke they were still there, walking around us in a circle, but always just beyond the edge of the clearing. A more terrifying bunch of fierce and bloodthirsty monsters it would be difficult to imagine. They wandered off into the jungle shortly after sunrise, and when we thought the last of them was gone, we resumed our journey.

Occasionally we caught glimpses of the horrid beasts during the day. Fortunately, we were never far from a meadow island, and their pursuit always ended at the verge of the solid sod.

Toward noon, we stumbled on a well-constructed road. I was confident that it led to one of the principal cities of Kaol. Just as we entered it from one side, a huge flying monster emerged from the jungle on the other side and charged us.

Imagine if you can, a hornet grown to the size of a bull, and you will have some idea of the

winged demon that flew down at me. My sword
seemed like a pitiful weapon against the beast's
frightful jaws and its large poisoned stinger. I did
not have a chance to escape its lightning-like
movements or hide from those many eyes that
covered three-fourths of its hideous head.

Even ferocious Woola was as helpless as a kitten compared to that frightful thing. But to flee
would be useless, so I stood my ground, Woola
snarling at my side. My only hope was to die as I
had always lived—fighting.

The creature was on us now, and at that
instant I saw a slight chance for survival. If I
could just remove the poison sacs that fed the
stinger, the struggle might be more equal. At the
thought, I called to Woola to leap up on the creature's head and hang there, and as his mighty
jaws closed on that fiendish head, and his glistening fangs buried themselves in the bone and car-
tilage and lower part of one of its huge eyes, I
snuck underneath as the creature rose, dragging
Woola up off the ground. I was able to see its
stinger and the rearmost body of the thing.

I was courting instant death by putting myself
in the path of that poison-laden stinger, but it was
the only way. As the thing shot toward me, I
swung my sword in a powerful cut that severed the
stinger where it joined the thing's body. Then, like
a battering ram, one of its powerful hind legs

caught me in the chest and knocked me clear across the broad highway and into the jungle. Fortunately, I passed between the trees! If I had hit one, I would have been badly injured, if not killed.

Though I was dazed, I stumbled to my feet and staggered back to help Woola. The savage thing was circling ten feet off the ground, beating at the calot with all six of its powerful legs. Even during my sudden flight through the air, I had not let go of my sword, and now I ran under the two battling monsters, jabbing it up at the winged terror with all my might.

The thing could easily have flown out of my reach, but it choose to stay and fight. It dropped down on me, and before I could escape had grabbed my shoulder in its powerful jaws. The now useless stub of its giant stinger struck me repeatedly, and the blows were almost as powerful as the kick of a horse! The thing would have hammered me to a pulp if not for a sudden stop to the hostilities.

From where I hung, a few feet above the road, I could see along the highway a few hundred feet and suddenly spotted a red warrior come into view from around the bend. He was mounted on a thoat, one of the smaller species used by red men, and he held a long, light lance.

His mount was walking sedately when I first spotted them, but the instant that the red man saw us, his thoat went into full charge. His long lance dipped down, and as thoat and rider charged under us, the lance was driven completely through the monster's body.

With a convulsive shudder, the thing stiffened, the jaws relaxed, and I dropped to the ground. I watched as the creature plunged onto the road right on top of Woola, who was still clinging to its gory head. By the time I got to my feet, the red man had turned and ridden back to us. Woola, finding his enemy inert and lifeless, released his hold and wriggled out from under the body.

I started to thank the stranger for his timely assistance, but he rudely cut me off as he demanded, "Who are you, who dare enter the land of Kaol and hunt in the royal forest of the jeddak?"

Then, as he noted my white skin through the coating of grime and blood that covered me, his eyes went wide, and in an altered tone he whispered: "Can it be that you are a Holy Thern?"

I considered trying to deceive the fellow, but I had thrown away the yellow wig and the holy headband in the presence of Matai Shang. I knew that it would not be long before my new acquaintance discovered he truth.

"I am not a Thern," I replied, and then, flinging caution to the winds, I said: "I am John

Carter, Prince of Helium, whose name may be known to you."

If his eyes had gone wide when he thought that I was a Holy Thern, they almost popped now that he knew that I was John Carter! I held my sword firmly as I spoke those words. I was afraid those might be fighting words, but to my surprise nothing happened.

"John Carter, Prince of Helium," he repeated slowly, as though he could not quite grasp the truth of the statement. "John Carter, the mightiest warrior of Barsoom!"

He then dismounted and placed his hand on my shoulder. This is the most friendly greeting on Mars. "It is my duty to kill you, John Carter, but I have always admired your fighting ability and believed in your sincerity. I question the Therns and do not believe in their religion.

"It would mean my death if this heresy was suspected in the court of Kulan Tith. I wish to serve you, Prince, you have only to command Torkar Bar, Captain of the Kaolian Road."

Truth and honesty were plain on the warrior's face, so I knew that I could trust him, even though he should have been my enemy. His title of Captain of the Kaolian Road explained his timely presence here. Almost every highway on Mars is patrolled by these noble warriors. There is hardly any service more honorable than this lonely and dangerous duty.

"Torkar Bar has already placed a great debt of gratitude upon my shoulders," I replied, pointing to the carcass of the creature he had just killed with his long spear.

The red man smiled and said, "It was fortunate that I came along. Only this poisoned spear can kill a sith quickly enough to save its prey. In this section of Kaol, we are all armed with a long sith spear, smeared with the sith's own poison. Nothing else acts so quickly on the beast as its own poison.

"Look," he continued, using his dagger to make an incision in the carcass a foot above the root of the sting. He then plucked out two sacs, each of which held a gallon of the deadly liquid.

"In the olden days, Kaol was overrun with these frightful monsters. They often came in herds of twenty or thirty, darting down into our cities from above and carrying away women, children, and even warriors."

I was wondering just how much I could safely tell this man of my mission, but his next words put me at ease, "And now as to yourself, John Carter, I shall not ask your business here, nor do I wish to hear it. I have eyes and ears and ordinary intelligence, and yesterday morning I saw the party that came to the city of Kaol from the north in a small flier. But I do ask your word that you contemplate no overt act against either the nation of Kaol or its jeddak."

"You have my word, Torkar Bar, and I thank you for your courtesy."

"My way leads along the Kaolian road, away from the city of Kaol," he continued. "I have seen no one—John Carter least of all. And you have not seen Torkar Bar. You understand?"

"Perfectly," I replied.

He laid his hand on my shoulder.

"This road leads directly into the city of Kaol," he said. "I wish you fortune," and vaulting to the back of his thoat he trotted away without a backward glance.

Woola and I spotted the wall that surrounds the city of Kaol just after dark. We had traveled the entire way without further mishap, and though the few folks we met on the road stared at the calot, no one detected the red pigment I had smeared over my body.

But crossing the empty country and entering the guarded city of Kulan Tith, Jeddak of Kaol, were two very different things. No man enters a Martian city without giving a very detailed account of himself. I did not believe I could trick the guard officers when I tried to enter.

I planned to sneak into the city quietly under cover of darkness and hide in some crowded area. With this idea in mind, I circled the city's wall, keeping inside the fringe of the forest, which was cut away from the wall for several hundred feet all around the city.

I tried to climb the wall at several different places, but not even my earthly muscles could overcome that cleverly constructed rampart with its strange slope and mirror-like finish.

Discouraged, I went back into the forest and lay down to sleep, with Woola resting beside me, standing watch.

CHAPTER 6

A Hero in Kaol

It was daylight when I awoke to the sound of movement nearby. As I opened my eyes, Woola moved and stared through the brush toward the road. At first I could see nothing, but soon caught a glimpse of something smooth and glossy moving through the multicolored vegetation.

Motioning Woola to stay where he was, I crept forward to investigate and saw a long line of the hideous green warriors of the dead sea bottoms hiding in the dense jungle beside the road. There could be but one explanation. The green men were waiting to ambush the next troop of red warriors leaving the city.

I owed no loyalty to the Jeddak of Kaol, but he was of the same race of noble red men as my own princess. I could not stand by and see his warriors butchered by the cruel and heartless green demons of Barsoom. I retraced my steps to where

I had left Woola and signaled him to follow me. Making a detour to avoid the chance of falling into the hands of the green men, I came to the wall.

A hundred yards to my right was the gate where I supposed the troops were expected to come out, but to reach it I had to pass in front of the green warriors. I feared that my plan to warn the Kaolians might be discovered, so I ran to the left, where another gate a mile away would give me entry into the city.

I knew that the word I brought would be a good passport into Kaol. If I could get inside the city's wall, there might be opportunity to disappear in the confusion and excitement that was sure to follow my announcement. In the turmoil I hoped to find my way to the palace of the jeddak, where I was sure Matai Shang and his party would be quartered.

I had just started in the direction of the far gate when the sound of marching troops, the clank of metal, and the squealing of thoats alerted me that the Kaolians were already moving toward the other gate. There was no time to be lost. In another moment the gate would be opened, and the head of the column would pass out onto the highway where death was waiting in the forest.

Turning back toward the gate, I ran along the edge of the clearing, covering the ground in the long leaps that had first made me famous on Barsoom. Thirty, fifty, a hundred feet at a bound are nothing for the muscles of an athletic Earthman on Mars.

As I passed in front of the waiting green men, they saw me and knew their trap had been discovered. Those nearest me jumped out to try to cut me off before I could reach the gate.

At the same instant, the gate swung wide open, and the head of the Kaolian column emerged. A dozen green warriors had succeeded in blocking my way to the gate. I did not slacken my speed as I dashed among them, and as they fell before my blade I recalled the happy memory of other battles on Barsoom. I remembered when Tars Tarkas, Jeddak of Thark, mightiest of Martian green men, stood beside me as we hewed down our enemies until the pile of corpses around us rose higher than a man's head.

When a group of them charged me in front of the Kaol gateway, I leaped over them, and copying the tactics of the hideous plant men of Dor, I swung at their heads as I passed above.

The red warriors were charging out of the city, and the savage horde of green men were coming out of the jungle to meet them. In a moment, I was in the center of a fierce and bloody battle.

The Kaolians were fearless fighters, and the

green men of the equator were just as warlike as their cold, cruel cousins of the temperate zone. There were times when either side could have withdrawn and ended the hostilities but that was not even considered. I realized that what might have been just a small skirmish would end with the complete extermination of one force or the other.

Once my joy of battle was aroused, I took delight in the fray. My fighting ability was noted by the Kaolians and was often rewarded by shouts of praise. If I sometimes seem to take too great pride in my fighting ability, it must be remembered that fighting is my vocation. If your vocation is shoeing horses, or painting pictures, and you can do one or the other better than anyone else, then you are a fool if you are not proud of your ability. Make no mistake, I am very proud that no greater fighter has ever lived than John Carter, Prince of Helium.

I outdid myself that day to impress that fact on the natives of Kaol! I wanted to win my way into their hearts—and their city. I was not disappointed in my desire. All day we fought, until the road was red with blood and clogged with corpses. Back and forth along the slippery highway the tide of battle surged, but the gateway to Kaol was never really in danger.

There were breathing spells when I had a chance to talk with the red men panting beside me, and once the jeddak, Kulan Tith himself, laid his hand on my shoulder and asked my name.

"I am Dotar Sojat," I replied, remembering a name given me by the Tharks many years before. It came from the family names of the first two of their warriors I had killed.

"You are a mighty warrior, Dotar Sojat," he replied, "and when this day is done, I want to speak with you again in my audience chamber."

And then the fight surged around us once more, and we were separated, but I knew I had achieved my goal. It was with renewed vigor and a joyous soul that I reentered the fight. I hacked wildly at every enemy until the last of the green men was killed or had left the field.

Not until the battle was over did I learn why the red troops had sallied forth that day. Kulan Tith was expecting a visit from a mighty jeddak of the North—a powerful ally of the Kaolians. It had been his wish to meet his guest a full day's journey from Kaol.

But now the march of the welcoming host was delayed until the following morning, when the troops again set out from Kaol. I had not been invited to meet Kulan Tith after the battle, but he had sent an officer to find me. I was escorted to spacious quarters in the palace set aside for officers of the royal guard.

Woola and I spent a comfortable night and

awoke refreshed after the arduous labors of the past few days. Neither of us had come through the conflict unscathed, but the marvelous, healing salves of Barsoom made us as good as new overnight.

I ate breakfast with a number of the Kaolian officers, whom I found courteous and delightful hosts. I had just finished my meal when a messenger arrived from Kulan Tith commanding my presence.

As I entered, the jeddak got up, stepped down from his magnificent throne, and came forward to meet me—a mark of distinction that is seldom accorded to anyone other than a visiting ruler.

"Kaor, Dotar Sojat!" he greeted me. "I have summoned you to receive the grateful thanks of the people of Kaol. If not for your heroic bravery in daring fate to warn us of the ambush, we would surely have fallen into their well-laid trap. Tell me more of yourself—from what country do you come, and what errand brings you to the court of Kulan Tith."

"I am from Hastor," I said, for I owned a small palace in that southern city which lies within the far-flung dominions of Helium.

"My presence in the land of Kaol is partly due to accident. My flier was wrecked on the southern fringe of your forest. It was while seeking entrance to the city of Kaol that I discovered the green horde lying in wait for your troops."

If Kulan Tith wondered what business brought me in a flier to the very edge of his domain, he was good enough not to press me further. I would have had difficulty in making up a story.

During my audience with the jeddak, another party entered the chamber from behind me. I did not see their faces until Kulan Tith stepped past me to greet them, commanding me to follow and be presented. As I turned around I could barely control my features, for there, listening to Kulan Tith's words praising me, stood my arch-enemies, Matai Shang and Thurid.

"Holy Hekkador of the Holy Therns," the jeddak was saying, "shower thy blessings on Dotar Sojat, the brave stranger from distant Hastor, whose wondrous heroism and marvelous ferocity saved the day for Kaol!"

Matai Shang stepped forward and laid his hand on my shoulder. There was no indication that he recognized me—I guessed that my disguise was complete. He spoke kindly to me and then presented me to Thurid. The black, too, apparently was deceived. Then Kulan Tith told them of my exploits on the field of battle.

The thing that seemed to have impressed him most was my remarkable agility. Time and again he described the amazing way I had leaped over an enemy, cleaving his skull wide open with my sword as I sailed above him.

I thought that I saw Thurid's eyes widen a bit during the narrative, and several times I caught him gazing intently at my face. Was he starting to suspect me? Then Kulan Tith talked about the savage calot that fought alongside me, and after that Matai Shang started looking at me with suspicion—or did I only imagine it?

At the close of the audience, Kulan Tith announced that I would accompany him on the way to meet his royal guest. I left with an officer who was to procure proper trappings and a suitable mount for me. I sighed with relief as we walked out of the chamber, praying that neither of my enemies suspected my true identity.

A half-hour later I rode out of the city with Kulan Tith and his warriors on the way to meet his friend and ally. Though my eyes and ears had been wide open during my audience with the jeddak and my various passages through the palace, I had seen or heard nothing of Dejah Thoris or Thuvia. I would have preferred to stay behind during Kulan Tith's absence, so I could search for them.

Toward noon we spotted the gorgeous train that accompanied the visiting jeddak. It stretched for miles along the wide, white road to Kaol.

Mounted troops, their trappings of jewel and metal-incrusted leather glistening in the sunlight, formed the vanguard of the body. After them came a thousand gorgeous chariots drawn by huge zitidars.

These low, commodious wagons moved stately down the road, and on either side of them marched solid ranks of mounted warriors protecting their occupants, the women and children of the royal court. On the back of each monster zitidar rode a Martian youth, and the whole scene carried me back to my first days on Barsoom. It was twenty-two years ago when I had first seen the gorgeous caravan of the green horde of Tharks.

I had never seen zitidars in the service of red men before today. These brutes are huge mastodon-like animals that tower to an immense height even beside the giant green men and their giant thoats. The beasts wore jeweled trappings and saddles of brightly colored silk, embroidered in fanciful designs with strings of diamonds, pearls, rubies, emeralds, and the countless unnamed jewels of Mars. Each chariot displayed a dozen streamers and flags that fluttered in the breeze.

Just in front of the chariots, the visiting jeddak rode alone on a pure white thoat—another unusual sight. After him came interminable ranks of mounted spearmen, riflemen, and swordsmen.

It was indeed a most imposing sight.

Except for the clanking of accoutrements and the occasional squeal of an angry thoat or the low growl of a zitidar, the passage of the cavalcade was almost noiseless. Neither thoat nor zitidar is a hoofed animal, and the broad tires of the chariots are of an elastic material that makes hardly any sound. Now and then the laughter of a woman or the chatter of children could be heard—the red Martians are a social, pleasure-loving people.

The meeting ceremonies of the two jeddaks consumed an hour, and then we turned and retraced our way toward the city of Kaol. The head of the column reached Kaol just before dark, though it must have been nearly morning before the rear guard passed through the gateway.

Fortunately, I was positioned well up toward the head of the column, and after the lavish banquet, which I attended with the officers of the royal guard, I was free to relax in my quarters. With the constant arrival of the officers of the visiting jeddak's retinue, there was so much activity in the palace that I did not attempt a search for Dejah Thoris.

As I passed along the corridors between the banquet hall and my quarters, I had a feeling someone was watching me. I turned around and caught a glimpse of a figure darting into an open doorway. Though I ran quickly back to the spot where he disappeared, I could find no trace of him. But I knew, even with the brief glimpse, that I had seen a white face topped with a mass of yellow hair.

The incident gave me food for thought. If I were right, then Matai Shang and Thurid must suspect my identity, and even the service I rendered Kulan Tith could not save me from their religious fanaticism. But vague conjecture and fruitless speculation never worried me enough to keep me from my rest, and I threw myself on my sleeping silks and furs and passed into dreamless slumber.

Calots were not permitted inside the palace, and so I had had to leave poor Woola in the stables where the royal thoats are kept. He had comfortable, even luxurious accomodations, but I would rather have had him with me. If he had been guarding me, the event that happened that night would not have come to pass.

I was jarred out of my sleep by some cold and clammy thing forced across my forehead. I jumped to my feet and grabbed at the fearsome thing. My hand touched human flesh, and then as I lunged in the darkness to seize this visitor, my foot got caught in my sleeping silks, and I fell to the floor.

By the time I got to my feet and turned on the light, my caller had disappeared. Careful search of the room revealed nothing to explain either the identity or business of the person who had been there. I could not believe it was a thief, since thieves are practically unknown on Barsoom. However, assassination is common, but even this could not have been his motive—he could easily have killed me if that was his desire.

I was just returning to sleep when a dozen Kaolian guardsmen entered my apartment. The officer in charge was one of my hosts that morning, but now his face showed no sign of friendship.

"Kulan Tith commands your presence!" he said. "Come!"

CHAPTER 7

New Allies

I was marched back to the great audience chamber in the center of the jeddak's palace. As I entered the room, filled with the nobles of Kaol and the officers of the visiting jeddak, all eyes turned my way. Up on the dais sat Kulan Tith and his two guests, Matai Shang and the visiting jeddak. We marched up to the foot of the thrones in deadly silence.

"Make your accusation," said Kulan Tith, turning to Thurid, the black dator of the First Born, as he stepped forward and faced me.

"Most noble Jeddak," he said, "I had suspicions about this stranger inside your palace. Your description of his fiendish skills compared with that of the arch-enemy of truth on Barsoom.

"But so there would be no mistake, I sent a priest of your own holy cult to make the test that would pierce his disguise and reveal the truth.

Behold the result!" Thurid shouted and pointed his finger at my forehead.

All eyes followed the direction of that accusing digit—I alone seemed at a loss to guess what they saw. The brows of Kulan Tith darkened in a menacing scowl as his eyes rested on my face, though I did not know why. But then the guard standing next to me took out a small mirror and held it in front of me.

One glance at the mirror showed that the sneaking Thern had reached out through the concealing darkness of my bed-chamber and wiped away a patch of my red pigment disguise. The tanned texture of my own white skin showed plainly. For a moment Thurid ceased speaking, to enhance, I suspect, the dramatic effect of his disclosure. Then he continued, "Here, O Kulan Tith, is he who has desecrated the temples of the Gods of Mars, who has violated the persons of the Holy Therns themselves, and turned a world against its age-old religion. Before you, in your power, Jeddak of Kaol, Defender of the Holies, stands John Carter, Prince of Helium!"

Kulan Tith looked toward Matai Shang as the Holy Thern nodded his head and tried to seal my doom as he said, "It is indeed the arch-blasphemer! Even now he has followed me to the very heart of your palace, Kulan Tith, for the sole purpose of assassinating me. He—"

"He lies!" I cried. "Kulan Tith, listen and you will know the truth. Listen while I tell you why John Carter has followed Matai Shang to the heart of your palace. Listen to me as well as to them, and then judge if my acts are not more in accord with true Barsoomian chivalry and honor! These men are merely revengeful devotees of the awful religion from whose cruel bonds I have freed your planet."

"Silence!" roared the jeddak, leaping to his feet and laying his hand on the hilt of his sword. "Silence, blasphemer! Kulan Tith does not need to permit the air of his audience chamber to be defiled by the heresies that issue from your polluted throat.

"You stand already self-condemned. I need only determine the manner of your death. Even the service that you rendered on the battlefield will not help you! I see now it was just a trick to win your way into my favor. To the pits with him!" he concluded, addressing the officer of my guard.

What a mess! What chance did I have against a whole nation? How could I hope for mercy at the hands of the fanatical Kulan Tith with such advisers as Matai Shang and Thurid? The black grinned hatefully in my face as he taunted, "You will not escape this time, Earth man!"

The guards closed toward me. A red haze blurred my vision. The fighting blood of my

Virginian ancestors coursed hot through my veins. The lust of battle was on me.

With a leap I was beside Thurid, and before the devilish smirk had faded from his handsome face, I had smashed him in the mouth with my clenched fist. As the good, old American blow landed, the black dator fell back to crumple in a heap at the foot of Kulan Tith's throne, spitting blood and teeth.

Then I drew my sword and swung around, on guard, to face a nation.

In an instant the guardsmen were on me, but before a blow had been struck a loud voice rose above the din of shouting warriors. A giant figure leaped from the dais and, with drawn sword, threw himself between me and my adversaries.

It was the visiting jeddak!

"Stop! Stop where your are!" he cried. "If you value my friendship, Kulan Tith and the age-old peace that has existed between our peoples, call off your swordsmen! Whoever fights John Carter, Prince of Helium, must also fight Thuvan Dihn, Jeddak of Ptarth!"

The shouting ceased and the menacing swords were lowered as a thousand eyes turned first toward Thuvan Dihn and then to Kulan Tith. At first the Jeddak of Kaol went white in rage, but before he spoke he got control of himself. His tone was calm and even and diplomatic as he addressed his friend, another great jeddak.

"Thuvan Dihn, you must have good reasons why you break the ancient customs which govern the deportment of a guest within the palace of his host. So that I do not forget myself as has my royal friend, I prefer to remain silent until the Jeddak of Ptarth has explained his action and related the causes which provoked it."

I could see that the Jeddak of Ptarth was of half a mind to throw his metal in Kulan Tith's face, but he controlled himself, as he replied, "No one knows the laws that govern the acts of men in the domains of their neighbors better than Thuvan Dihn. But Thuvan Dihn owes allegiance to a higher law than these—the law of gratitude. And to no man on Barsoom does he owe a greater debt of gratitude than to John Carter, Prince of Helium.

"Years ago, Kulan Tith, during your last visit to my realm, you were greatly taken with the charms and graces of my only daughter, Thuvia. You saw how I adored her, and later you learned that, inspired by some whim, she had taken the last, long, voluntary pilgrimage on the cold River Iss, leaving me desolate.

"Some months ago, I heard of the expedition which John Carter had led against Issus and the Holy Therns. I had heard rumors of the atrocities committed by the Therns against the pilgrims but did not believe them.

"Then I heard that thousands of prisoners had been released, but only a few dared return to their own countries. They could not face the terrible death which is mandated for all who return from the Valley Dor.

"I still kept to the old religion, and I prayed that my daughter Thuvia would die before she committed the sacrilege of returning to the outer world. But then the love a father for his daughter asserted itself, and I vowed that if she could be found, I would prefer eternal damnation rather than be separated from her.

"So I sent emissaries to Helium and to the court of Xodar, Jeddak of the First Born, who now rules those of the Thern nation that have renounced their religion. From each of them I heard the same story of unspeakable cruelties and atrocities perpetrated upon the poor defenseless victims of their religion by the Holy Therns.

"There were many who had seen my daughter, and from Therns who had been close to Matai Shang, I learned of the indignities that he personally heaped upon her. I was pleased when I came here to find that Matai Shang was also your guest, for I planned to search him out for an accounting of his actions.

"I also heard of the chivalrous kindness that John Carter had accorded my daughter. They told me how he fought for her life, and how he rescued her from the Therns. They told me how he tried to return her to my court after their escape from the Valley Dor. Even when they were attacked by the savage Warhoons, he stayed behind to fight the green warriors after sending her off on his thoat to escape.

"Kulan Tith, is it any wonder that I am willing to jeopardize my life, the peace of my nation, or even your friendship, which I prize more than anything else, to protect the Prince of Helium?"

For a moment Kulan Tith was silent. I could see by the expression of his face that he was in a dilemma. Then he spoke, "Thuvan Dihn, who am I to judge my fellowman? In my eyes, the Father of Therns is still holy, and the religion which he teaches is still the only true religion. But if I were faced by the same problem as you, I have no doubt that I would feel and act precisely as you have.

"With the Prince of Helium I will act according to my desire, but between you and Matai Shang, I offer to help in reconciliation.

"The Prince of Helium shall be escorted in safety to the boundary of my domain before the next sunset, where he shall be free to go; but upon pain of death must he never again enter the land of Kaol.

"If there is a quarrel between you and the Father of Therns, I ask that you settle it after both of you have passed beyond the limits of my power. Are you satisfied, Thuvan Dihn?"

The Jeddak of Ptarth nodded his assent, but the ugly scowl that he directed at Matai Shang showed that pasty-faced false priest he was in for a lot of trouble.

"The Prince of Helium is far from satisfied!" I cried, interrupting this peaceful talk. I had no stomach for peace at the price that had been named.

"I have escaped death in a dozen forms to catch Matai Shang, and I do not intend to be meekly led away from the goal that I have won by my sword arm.

"Nor will Thuvan Dihn, Jeddak of Ptarth, be satisfied when he has heard me through. Do you know why I have followed Matai Shang and Thurid from the forests of the Valley Dor across half a world through almost insurmountable difficulties?

"Do you think that John Carter, Prince of Helium, would stoop to assassination? Could Kulan Tith believe that lie, whispered in his ear by the Holy Thern or Dator Thurid?

"I do not follow Matai Shang to kill him, though the God of my own planet knows that my hands itch to be at his throat. I follow him because he has two prisoners—my wife, Dejah Thoris, Princess of Helium, and your daughter, Thuvia of Ptarth.

"Do you think that I will permit myself to be

led beyond the walls of Kaol unless the mother of my son accompanies me, and your daughter is restored to your loving arms?"

Thuvan Dihn turned to Kulan Tith. Rage flamed in his keen eyes, but he kept his self-control as he spoke. "Did you know of this, Kulan Tith?" he asked. "Did you know that my daughter was a prisoner in your palace?"

"He could not know it," interrupted Matai Shang, white with what I am sure was more fear than rage. "He could not know it, for it is a lie."

I would have had his life for that on the spot, but even as I sprang toward him, Thuvan Dihn laid a heavy hand on my shoulder.

"Wait," he said to me, and then he spoke to Kulan Tith, "It is not a lie. This much have I learned of the Prince of Helium—he does not lie! Answer me, Kulan Tith—I have asked you a question."

"Three women came with the Father of Therns," replied Kulan Tith. "Phaidor, his daughter, and two who were reported to be her slaves. If these two are Thuvia of Ptarth and Dejah Thoris of Helium I did not know—I have seen neither of them. But if they are, then they shall be returned to you tomorrow."

As he spoke, he looked straight at Matai Shang, not as a devotee should look at a high priest, but as a ruler of men looks at one to whom he issues a command.

It must have been plain to the Father of Therns, as it was to me, that the recent disclosures of his true character had done much to weaken the faith of Kulan Tith. Matai Shang knew that it would require only a little more to turn the powerful jeddak into a dangerous enemy. But he also knew that the seeds of superstition are so strong that even the great Kaolian still hesitated to cut the final strand that bound him to his ancient religion.

Matai Shang was wise enough to seem to accept the mandate of his follower and promised to bring the two slave women to the audience chamber tomorrow. "It is almost morning now," he said, "and I do not want to disturb the slumber of my daughter. If not for that I would have them fetched at once so you could see that the Prince of Helium is mistaken."

I was about to object to any delay and demand that the Princess of Helium be brought to me immediately, when Thuvan Dihn made such insistence seem unnecessary. "I should like to see my daughter at once," he said, "but if Kulan Tith will give me his assurance that no one will be permitted to leave the palace tonight, and that no harm will come to either Dejah Thoris or Thuvia of Ptarth between now and the moment they are brought into our presence in this chamber at daylight, I shall not insist."

"No one will leave the palace tonight,"

replied the Jeddak of Kaol, "and Matai Shang will give us assurance that no harm will come to the two women?"

The Thern assented with a nod. A few moments later Kulan Tith indicated that the audience was at an end. At Thuvan Dihn's invitation, I accompanied the Jeddak of Ptarth to his own apartments, where we sat until daylight. He listened to the account of my experiences and to all that had befallen his daughter during the time that we had been together.

I found Thuvia's father to be a man after my own heart, and that night was the beginning of a friendship that has grown until it is second only to the one between Tars Tarkas, the green Jeddak of Thark, and myself.

The first burst of Mars's sudden dawn brought messengers from Kulan Tith, summoning us to the audience chamber where Thuvan Dihn was to receive his daughter after years of separation, and I was to be reunited with the glorious daughter of Helium after an almost unbroken separation of twelve years.

My heart pounded, and my arms ached to hold my lady whose eternal youth and undying beauty were just an outward manifestation of a perfect soul. At last the messenger sent to fetch Matai Shang returned. I craned my neck to catch the first glimpse of those who should be following, but the messenger was alone. Halting before the throne he addressed his jeddak in a voice that was plainly audible to all within the chamber.

"O Kulan Tith, Mightiest of Jeddaks," he cried, after the fashion of the court, "your messenger returns alone, for when he reached the apartments of the Father of Therns he found them empty!"

Kulan Tith went white.

A low groan burst from Thuvan Dihn's lips as he stood next to me. For a moment, the silence of death reigned in the great audience chamber of Kulan Tith, Jeddak of Kaol. It was he who broke the spell.

Rising from his throne, he stepped down from the dais to the side of Thuvan Dihn. Tears dimmed his eyes as he placed both hands on the shoulders of his friend.

"O Thuvan Dihn," he cried, "that this should have happened in the palace of your best friend! With my own hands would I have wrung the neck of Matai Shang if I had guessed what was in his foul heart. Last night my lifelong faith was weakened—this morning it has been shattered—but too late, too late.

"I will do anything to help you seize your daughter and the wife of this royal warrior from the clutches of these archfiends. You have command of the resources of a mighty nation, for all

Kaol is at your disposal. What may be done? Say the word!"

"First," I suggested, "let us find those of your people who are responsible for the escape of Matai Shang and his followers. Without assistance on the part of the palace guard, this could not have come to pass. Seek the guilty, and from them force an explanation of the manner of their going and the direction they have taken."

Before Kulan Tith could issue the commands that would start the investigation, a handsome young officer stepped forward and addressed his jeddak. "O Kulan Tith, Mightiest of Jeddaks," he said, "I alone am responsible for this grievous error. Last night I commanded the palace guard. I was on duty in other parts of the palace during the audience of the early morning and knew nothing of what transpired.

"The Father of Therns summoned me and explained that it was your wish that his party be escorted quickly from the city. He told me there was a deadly enemy here who sought the Holy Hekkador's life. I did only what a lifetime of training has taught me was the proper thing to do—I obeyed him whom I believed to be the ruler of us all, mightier even than you, mightiest of jeddaks.

"Let the consequences and the punishment fall on me alone, for I alone am guilty. Those others of the palace guard who assisted in the flight did so under my instructions."

Kulan Tith looked first at me and then at Thuvan Dihn, as though to ask our judgment, but the error was so innocent that neither of us had any mind to see the young officer suffer.

"How did they leave? What direction did they take?" asked Thuvan Dihn.

"They left as they came, on their own flier. For some time after they left I watched the vessel's lights, which finally vanished as they headed due north."

"Where in the North could Matai Shang find asylum?" asked Thuvan Dihn.

For some moments the Jeddak of Kaol stood with bowed head, apparently deep in thought. Then his face lit up and he cried, "I have it! Only yesterday Matai Shang told me of a race of people who dwell far to the North. He said they had always been known to the Holy Therns and were devout and faithful followers of the ancient cult. Among them would he find a perpetual haven of refuge, where no 'lying heretics' could find him. Matai Shang must have gone there!"

"May I use a flier from your air forces?" I cried.

"No, their whole fleet is training with mine in the outer regions, and none is nearer than Ptarth," replied Thuvan Dihn.

"Wait! Beyond the southern fringe of your forest lies the wreck of the flier which brought me here. If you will loan me men to fetch it, and mechanics to assist me, I can repair it in two days," I almost shouted, yearning to get this action started.

I had been a little suspicious of the Kaolian jeddak's sudden rejection of his religion, but the speed with which he embraced my suggestion, and the quickness with which a force of officers and men were placed at my disposal, removed my doubts.

Two days later, the flier rested on top of the watchtower, ready to depart. Thuvan Dihn and Kulan Tith had offered me the entire resources of their two nations—millions of fighting men were at my disposal. But my flier could hold only one man other than myself and Woola.

As I stepped aboard, Thuvan Dihn quickly took the place beside me. I looked at him with surprise, but he settled in like he knew what he was doing. He turned to his second in command and said, "To you I entrust the return of the convoy and my family to Ptarth. The Prince of Helium shall not go alone into the land of his enemies. I have spoken. Farewell!"

CHAPTER 8

Through the Carrion Caves

We flew straight north, our destination compass directing our path after the speeding flier. Day and night we followed, until early in the second night, we noticed the air becoming colder, and from the distance we had come from the equator, we knew we were rapidly approaching the North Arctic region.

I knew of many expeditions that had attempted to explore the unknown northern land. Not one had ever returned after passing the ice barrier that marks the southern border. What became of them no one knew—only that they passed out of sight into that grim and mysterious country of the North Pole.

The distance from the barrier to the Pole was no more than a swift flier could cover in a few hours, so it was assumed that some frightful catastrophe awaited those who reached the "forbidden land," as it had come to be called by the Martians of the outer world.

I went more slowly as we approached the barrier. I wanted to move cautiously over the frozen wasteland to get ample warning before I ran into an ambush. I knew Matai Shang was searching for a spot where he might feel secure from John Carter, Prince of Helium, and would take precautions.

We were flying at a snail's pace only a few feet above the ground—literally feeling our way through the darkness. Both moons had set, and the night was dark because of cloud cover.

Suddenly a towering wall of white rose directly in our path! I threw the helm hard over and reversed our engine, but I was too late! We hit with a sickening crash. The flier reeled over, the engine stopped, the patched buoyancy tanks burst, and we plunged headfirst twenty feet to the ground.

Fortunately, none of us was injured, and when we had disentangled ourselves from the wreckage, and the lesser moon had risen from below the horizon, we found that we were at the foot of a mighty ice barrier that stretched as far as we could see in either direction. What fate! With the journey all but completed, we were wrecked on the wrong side of an immensely high wall of ice! I looked at Thuvan Dihn as he shook his head dejectedly. We spent the rest of the night shivering in our inadequate sleeping silks and furs.

With daylight, my battered spirits regained something of their accustomed hopefulness, though I must admit that there was little for them to feed upon.

"What shall we do?" asked Thuvan Dihn. "How can we get past this impassable barrier?"

I replied, "I will not admit that it is impassable until I have followed its entire length and stand again upon this spot, defeated. The sooner we start, the better! I see no other way, and it will take us more than a month to travel the weary, frigid miles that lie before us."

For five days of cold and suffering, we covered the rough and frozen path that lies at the foot of the ice barrier. Fierce, fur-bearing creatures attacked us by day and night. We were never safe from the sudden charge of some huge demon of the North.

The apt was our most consistent and dangerous foe. It is a huge, white-furred creature with six limbs. Its four legs, short and heavy, carry it swiftly over the snow and ice; while the other two, growing forward from its shoulders on either side of its long, powerful neck, terminate in white, hairless hands.

Its head and mouth are more similar to a hippopotamus than to any other earthly animal, except that from the sides of the lower jawbone two large, sharp horns curve slightly downward.

Its two huge eyes inspired my greatest curiosity. They extend in two vast, oval patches from the center of the top of the cranium down either side of the head to below the roots of the horns, so that the horns seem to grow out from the lower part of the eyes.

After the fifth day we surprised the largest apt that we had seen. The creature stood fully eight feet at the shoulder and was so sleek and clean and glossy that he looked like he had recently been groomed. He stood eyeing us as we approached him. We knew it was a waste of time trying to escape the rage that seems to possess these creatures. They rove all over the dismal North, attacking every living thing that comes within range of their far-seeing eyes.

Even when their bellies are full, they kill for pleasure. When this particular apt failed to charge us, I was surprised until I saw the sheen of a golden collar around its neck as he turned and trotted away.

Thuvan Dihn saw it too, and it carried the same message of hope to both of us. Only man could have placed that collar there, and no race of Martians we knew had attempted to domesticate the ferocious apt. This one must belong to the people of the North—possibly to the fabled yellow men of Barsoom. This was a once powerful race that was supposed to be extinct, though some scholars thought they might still exist in this barren land.

We started down the trail of the great beast. Woola understood our desires, so we did not attempt to keep the animal in sight. Only Woola could follow it's swift flight over the rough ground, and soon they were both out of sight.

For two hours, the trail paralleled the ice barrier, and then it suddenly turned toward it through the roughest country I had ever seen. Enormous granite boulders blocked the way, deep rifts in the ice threatened to engulf us at the least misstep, and from the north a slight breeze brought an unspeakable stench that almost choked us.

For another two hours, we were occupied in covering a few hundred yards to the foot of the barrier. Then, turning around the corner of a wall-like outcropping of granite, we came to a smooth area of two or three acres in front of the base of the towering pile of ice and rock. After a quick examination, we saw the dark mouth of a cave.

The horrid stench was coming out of this opening! As Thuvan Dihn checked out the place, he halted with an exclamation of astonishment. "By all my ancestors!" he yelled. "These may be the fabled Carrion Caves! If so, we have found a way through the ice barrier.

"The ancient chronicles of Barsoom—so ancient that we have for ages considered them mythology—record the escape of the yellow men from the ravages of the green hordes. The green men overran Barsoom as the great oceans dried up and drove the dominant races from their strongholds.

"They tell of the wanderings of this once powerful race, harassed at every step, until at last they found a way through the ice barrier of the North to a fertile valley at the Pole.

"At the opening to the subterranean passage that led to their haven of refuge, a mighty battle was fought in which the yellow men were victorious. Inside the caves leading to their new home, they piled the bodies of the dead, both yellow and green, so that the stench might warn away their enemies from further pursuit.

"And ever since, the dead of this fabled land have been carried to the Carrion Caves, so that in death and decay they serve their country and warn away invading enemies. Here, too, is brought, so the fable runs, all the waste stuff of the nation—everything that is subject to rot and can add to the foul stench.

"And death lurks at every step among the rotting dead, for here the fierce apts make their lair, adding to the putrid accumulation with the fragments of their own prey which they cannot devour. It is a horrid avenue to our goal, but it is the only one."

"You are sure we have found the way to the land of the yellow men?" I cried.

"As sure as I may be, having only ancient legend to support my belief. But see how closely each detail tallies with the old story of the journey of the yellow race."

"If it is true then we may solve the mystery of the disappearance of Tardos Mors, Jeddak of Helium, and Mors Kajak, his son. No other spot on Barsoom has remained unexplored by the many expeditions and the countless spies that have been searching for them for nearly two years. The last word that came from them was that they sought Carthoris, my own brave son, beyond the ice barrier."

As we talked, we had been approaching the entrance to the cave, and as we crossed the threshold, I ceased to wonder that the ancient green enemies of the yellow men had been halted by these horrors.

The bones of dead men lay on the broad floor of the first cave, and over all was a putrid mush of decaying flesh. The apts had beaten a hideous trail through this mess toward the entrance to the second cave.

The entrance of this first cave was low so that the foul odors were confined and condensed to such an extent it seemed you could almost touch it. One was almost tempted to draw his dagger and hack his way through in search of pure air.

"Can we breathe this polluted air and live?" asked Thuvan Dihn, choking.

"Not for long, I imagine," I replied. "I will go first, and you bring up the rear, with Woola between. Come." And with these words, I dashed forward across the putrid mass. It was not until we had passed through seven of these stinking caves that we met with any physical opposition. Then, inside the eighth cave, we came to a lair of apts.

Twelve of the beasts were spread around the dark chamber. Some were sleeping, while others fought with each other as they tore at newly killed carcasses of their prey. Here in the dim light of their subterranean home, the value of their large eyes was obvious. These inner caves are shrouded in gloom that is almost utter darkness.

To attempt to pass through the midst of that fierce herd would be impossible, so I asked Thuvan Dihn to return to the outer world with Woola. I wanted the two of them to find their way to civilization and come back with enough men and equipment to overcome not only the apts, but any other obstacles that might lie between us and our goal.

"In the meantime," I continued, "I will try to discover some means of traveling alone to the land of the yellow men, but if I fail only one life will be sacrificed. If we all go on and perish, there will be no one to guide a rescue party to Dejah Thoris and your daughter."

"I shall not leave you here alone, John Carter," replied Thuvan Dihn firmly. "Whether you go on to victory or death, the Jeddak of Ptarth remains at your side. I have spoken."

I knew from his tone that it was useless to argue, so I decided to send Woola back with a note enclosed in a small metal case fastened to a harness around his neck. I commanded the faithful creature to seek Carthoris at Helium, and though half a world and countless dangers were on the way, I knew that if the thing could be done, Woola would do it.

I knew he was equipped by nature with marvelous speed and endurance and with frightful ferocity that made him a match for any single enemy. I hoped his keen intelligence and instinct would furnish everything else that was needed for the successful completion of his mission.

The great beast reluctantly turned to leave, but before he took off, I could not resist throwing my arms around his neck in a parting hug. He rubbed his cheek against mine in a final caress, and a moment later was speeding through the Carrion Caves toward the outer world.

In my note, I gave directions for locating the Carrion Caves. I told him not to attempt to fly over the ice barrier with a fleet. I told him I did not know what was beyond the eighth cave, but I was sure that somewhere on the other side, his mother was in the power of Matai Shang. I also said it was possible that his grandfather and great-grandfather were in the country as well.

Further, I advised him to call on Kulan Tith and the son of Thuvan Dihn and ask for enough warriors and ships to insure success at the first attack.

I concluded with, "Bring Tars Tarkas with you, for if I live until you reach me, I can think of few greater pleasures than to fight once more alongside my old friend."

After Woola bounded off, Thuvan Dihn and I discussed many plans for crossing the eighth chamber. From where we stood, we saw that the fighting among the apts was growing less, and that many had bedded down to sleep. It became apparent that soon all the ferocious monsters might be peacefully slumbering, and then we would have an opportunity to cross through their lair.

One by one, the remaining brutes stretched themselves out on the bubbling decomposition that covered the floor of their den, until only a single apt remained awake. This huge fellow roamed restlessly about, nosing among his companions and the revolting litter of the cave.

Occasionally he would stop to peer intently

toward first one of the exits from the chamber and then the other. He seemed to be acting like a sentry. We saw he was not going to sleep, so we tried to think of some way to trick him. I suggested a plan to Thuvan Dihn, and we decided to give it a try.

Thuvan Dihn hid just outside the entrance to the lair, while I deliberately showed myself to the guardian apt. The monstrous beast quickly moved toward us to investigate as I dashed back out and stood on the opposite side of the entrance looking straight at my partner.

As the apt poked his head through the narrow aperture that connected the caves, two swords were waiting for him, one on either side of the entrance. Before he even had an opportunity to growl, his severed head rolled at our feet.

Quickly we glanced into the chamber—not an apt had moved. Crawling over the carcass of the huge beast that blocked the doorway, we cautiously entered the dangerous den. We were like snails as we wound our way among the huge, sleeping forms leaving fresh tracks in the ooze behind us. The only sound louder than our breathing was the sucking noise as we waded through the muck of decaying flesh.

Halfway across the chamber a beast moved restlessly at the very instant I tried to step over him. I waited breathlessly, balancing on one foot!

I did not dare move a muscle! In my right hand was my keen dagger, the point hovering an inch above his savage heart.

Finally the apt relaxed, sighing, like at the end of a bad dream and resumed the regular respiration of deep slumber. I planted my raised foot on the other side of the fierce head and stepped over the beast.

Thuvan Dihn followed along behind me, and a short time later we were at the far opening. The Carrion Caves consist of a series of twenty-seven connecting chambers, and we moved through the remaining caverns without adventure or mishap.

We later learned that only once a month is it possible to find all the apts of the Carrion Caves in a single chamber. At other times they roam singly or in pairs in and out of the caves. It would have been impossible for two men to pass through the chambers without encountering an apt in nearly every one of them. Once a month they sleep for a full day, and it was our good fortune to choose the right time.

As we left the last cave, we emerged into a desolate country of snow and ice, but found a well-marked trail leading north. The path traveled around large boulders, so we only could see a short distance ahead of us. After a couple of hours, we passed around a huge boulder to come to a steep slope leading down into a valley. We spotted six men on the path—fierce, black-bearded fellows, with skins the color of a ripe lemon.

"The yellow men of Barsoom!" whispered Thuvan Dihn. He sounded amazed that the very race we expected to find hidden in this inaccessible land really did exist. We hid and watched the actions of the party as they stood at the foot of another huge rock with their backs toward us. One of them was peering around the edge of the granite mass as he watched someone approaching from the far side.

We soon got a clear view of another yellow man approaching us. All of these folk were clothed in magnificent furs—the six in the black and yellow striped hide of the orluk, while the one who approached alone was dazzling in the pure white skin of an apt.

The yellow men were armed with two swords, and a short javelin was slung across each man's back. Their left arms supported cuplike shields no larger than a dinner plate, with the concave sides turned outward toward an antagonist. They seemed puny implements of safety against a swordsman, but I was later to see their purpose and how well they could be used.

One of the swords carried by each warrior caught my immediate attention. I call it a sword, but really it was a sharp-edged blade with a hook at the far end. The other sword was straight and two-edged and about the same length as the hooked instrument. In addition to these weapons, each man carried a dagger in his harness.

As the white-furred one approached, the six held their swords more firmly—the hooked instrument in the left hand, the straight sword in the right, while above the left wrist the small shield was held rigid by a metal bracelet.

As the lone warrior came into view, the six attacked him with fiendish yells that sounded just like the savage war-cry of the Apaches of the American Southwest. Instantly, the attacked man drew both his swords, and as the six charged him, I witnessed as fierce a fight as one might care to see. With their sharp hooks, the combatants attempted to take hold of an adversary, but the cup-shaped shield was used to trap the darting weapon into its hollow. We watched in amazement as the lone warrior caught an attacker in the side with his hook, drew him in close, and ran him through with his sword.

But the odds were too unequal, and though the one who fought alone was by far the best and bravest of them all, it was only a question of time before the remaining five would find an opening and bring him down.

My sympathies have always been with the

weaker side of an argument. Even though I knew nothing about this fight, I could not stand by and see a brave man butchered by superior numbers. So before Thuvan Dihn knew what I was doing, he saw me standing by the side of the white-clad yellow man, battling like mad with his five remaining adversaries.

CHAPTER 9

With the Yellow Men

Thuvan Dihn joined us immediately, and though we found the hooked weapon a strange and savage thing to deal with, the three of us soon killed the five black-bearded warriors. When the battle was over, our new acquaintance removed the shield from his wrist and held it out to me. I did not know the significance of his act, but judged that it was a form of expressing his gratitude. I learned later that it symbolized the offering of a man's life in return for some great favor. My act of refusing this gift was the appropriate response.

"Then accept from Talu, Prince of Marentina, this token of my gratitude," he said as he reached beneath one of his wide sleeves and brought out a bracelet and placed it on my arm. He then went through the same ceremony with Thuvan Dihn.

Next he asked our names and from what land we hailed. He seemed quite familiar with the geography of the outer world, and when I said I was from Helium he raised his brows and said, "Ah, you seek your ruler and his company?"

"Do you know anything about them?" I asked quickly.

"I know little more than that they were captured by my uncle, Salensus Oll, Jeddak of Jeddaks, Ruler of Okar, land of the yellow men. As to their fate I know nothing, for I am at war with my uncle, who wants to crush my power in Marentina.

"These brutes we have slain are warriors he has sent out to assassinate me. It is well known that I often come out here alone to hunt the sacred apt. It is partly because I hate his religion that Salensus Oll is after me; but mostly he fears my growing power. He knows that many throughout Okar would be glad to see me as their new ruler and Jeddak of Jeddaks in his place.

"He is a cruel tyrant loathed by almost everyone. If it was not for the terror he has caused, and for the great fear the people have of him, I could raise an army overnight that would wipe out the few that might remain loyal to him. My own people are faithful to me, and the little valley of Marentina has paid no tribute to the court of Salensus Oll for a year.

"We are safe behind our mountain passes, a dozen of my men could hold the narrow way to Marentina against a million. But now, let us talk of your affairs. How may I aid you? My palace is at your disposal if you wish to honor me by coming to Marentina."

"When our work is done we shall be glad to accept your invitation," I replied. "But now you can assist us most by directing us to the court of Salensus Oll. We also want your thoughts on how we can gain admission to the city and the palace, or whatever other place we might find our friends."

Talu gazed at our smooth faces and at Thuvan Dihn's red skin and then at my white features. "First you must come to Marentina! A change must be made in your appearance before you can hope to enter any city in Okar. You must have yellow faces and black beards, and your apparel and trappings must be those that will not arouse suspicion. In my palace is one who can make you appear just like true yellow men."

His counsel seemed wise, and since we knew no other way to make a successful entry to Kadabra, the capital city of Okar, we set out with our new friend for his little, rock-bound country.

The way was over some of the worst country I have ever seen. It is no wonder that in this land where there are neither thoats nor fliers that

Marentina has little fear of invasion. At last, from a slight elevation a half-mile away, we got our first view of the city.

The peaceful little city lay nestled in a deep valley. I was amazed to see that the entire city, every street and plaza and open space, was roofed over with glass. All around was snow and ice, but there was none on the rounded, domelike, crystal covering that protected this city. As I was later to learn, all the other Marentina cities are also covered with similar domes.

Then I saw how these people coped with the rigors of the arctic and lived in luxury and comfort in the midst of a land of perpetual ice. The city was a veritable hothouse, and once I was inside, my respect and admiration for the scientific and engineering skill of this nation knew no bounds.

The moment we entered the city, Talu threw off his outer garments, and we followed his example. I saw that his apparel differed little from that of the red races of Barsoom. Except for his leather harness, thickly covered with jewels and metal, he was naked, nor could one have comfortably worn apparel in that warm and humid atmosphere.

For three days we remained the guests of Prince Talu, and during that time, he showered us with every attention and courtesy at his power.

He showed us all that was of interest in his great city.

We started with the Marentina atmosphere plant that will maintain life indefinitely in the cities of the North Pole. They are independent of any other air supply. Our tour reminded me of the central atmosphere plant that once ceased functioning. That event gave me the opportunity of restoring life and happiness to this strange world that I had already learned to love so well.

He showed us the heating system that stores the sun's rays in great reservoirs beneath the city and how little is necessary to maintain the perpetual summer heat of the glorious garden spot inside this arctic paradise.

Broad grassy avenues carried the noiseless traffic of light and airy ground fliers that are the only form of transportation used north of the gigantic ice barrier.

The broad tires of these unique fliers are rubber-like gas bags filled with the eighth Barsoomian ray, or ray of propulsion. It is this ray that propels the reflected light of the planet off into space and when confined gives the Martian craft their buoyancy.

The ground fliers of Marentina contain just enough buoyancy in their automobile-like wheels to give the cars traction for steering purposes. The rear wheels are geared to the engine and aid in driving the machine. A propeller at the stern does the main part of the propulsion work of these vehicles.

It is a delightful sensation, riding in one of these luxuriously appointed cars as they skim, light and airy as feathers, along the soft, mossy avenues of Marentina. They move quietly between the borders of their crimson path and beneath arching trees gorgeous with the wondrous blooms that are characteristic of Barsoomian vegetation.

By the end of the third day, the court barber—I can think of no other earthly name to describe him—had made such a remarkable transformation in both Thuvan Dihn and myself that our own wives would never have known us. Our skins were now a lemon color, and full, black beards and mustaches had been glued to our smooth faces. We wore the trappings of Okar warriors, and we each had black and yellow orluk suits for wear outside the hothouse cities.

Talu gave us careful directions for the journey to Kadabra. This good friend even accompanied us part way toward our goal. As we parted, he gave me a ring set with a dead-black, lusterless stone, which looked more like a bit of coal than the priceless Barsoomian gem which it really is.

"There were only three other stones cut from the mother stone. These three are worn by nobles high in my confidence who have been sent on secret missions to the court of Salensus Oll. Now you have the fourth.

"If you come within fifty feet of any of these three stones you will feel a rapid, pricking sensation in your ring finger. The man who wears its mate will experience the same feeling. It is caused by an electrical action that takes place the moment two of these gems come close to each other. You will know that a friend is close by.

"If another wearer of one of these gems calls for help, you must give him support. Guard this ring with your life, John Carter, for some day it may mean more than life to you."

With these parting words our good friend turned back toward Marentina, and we set off toward the city of Kadabra and the court of Salensus Oll, Jeddak of Jeddaks.

That very evening we came within sight of the walled and glass-roofed city. It lies in a low depression near the Pole, surrounded by rocky, snow-clad hills. From the pass, we had a splendid view of this great city of the North. Its crystal domes sparkled in the brilliant sunlight gleaming above the frost-covered outer wall that circles the entire one hundred miles of its circumference.

Large gates allowed entrance to the city at regular intervals, but we could see that all of them were closed at this time. Following Talu's suggestion, we were prepared to wait until morning to enter the city.

We found numerous caves in the hillsides around us and crept into one for the night. Our warm orluk skins kept us comfortable, and after a refreshing sleep, we awoke shortly after daylight on the following morning.

The city was already active at this hour, and we saw parties of yellow men emerging from several of the gates. Following our instructions, we stayed concealed for several hours until a party of six warriors passed along the trail below our hiding place.

After giving them time to get away from our cave, we crept out and followed them. When we were close enough behind them, I called out to their leader. The whole party stopped and turned toward us, and we knew the crucial test had come. If we could deceive these men we hoped the rest would be easy.

"Kaor!" I cried out as I came closer to them.

"Kaor!" responded the officer in charge.

"We come from Illall," I continued, giving the name of the most remote city of Okar, which has little interface with Kadabra. "We arrived yesterday, and this morning the captain of the gate told us that you were setting out to hunt orluks. This is a sport we do not find around our own city, and we ask that you allow us to accompany your hunting party."

The officer permitted us to go with them for the day. The guess that they were off on an orluk hunt proved correct. Talu had said that the chances were very good that anyone leaving Kadabra by the pass where we waited would be on a hunting trip. The pass leads directly to the plains where this large elephant-like beast of prey roams.

In so far as the hunt was concerned, the day was a failure. We did not see a single orluk, but this proved fortunate for us. The yellow men were so embarrassed by their misfortune that they would not reenter the city by the same gate where they left in the morning. It seemed that they had made many boasts to the captain of that gate about their skill at this dangerous sport. I was relieved that I would not have to talk with the captain who "directed" us to these hunters.

We had come quite close to the city when my attention was attracted to a tall, black shaft that rose up in the air several hundred feet from what appeared to be a tangled mass of junk at its base. I did not want to ask about it for fear of arousing suspicion. But before we reached the city gate I was to learn the purpose of the grim shaft and the meaning of the accumulation beneath it.

We were almost at the gate when one of the party called out, pointing toward the southern horizon. Following his lead, I spotted the hull of a large flier approaching rapidly.

"More fools who would solve the mysteries of the forbidden north," said the officer, half to himself. "Will they never stop their fatal curiosity?"

"Let us hope not! What would we do for slaves and sport if not for these new victims?" answered one of the warriors.

"True—but what stupid beasts they are to continue to come to a region from where none of them has ever returned."

"Let us stop and watch the show."

The officer looked toward the city. "The watch has seen him," he said, "we should remain. We may be needed."

I looked toward the city and saw several hundred warriors leaving from the nearest gate. They moved leisurely, as though there were no need for haste.

Then I turned my eyes once more toward the flier. She was moving rapidly toward the city, and when she had come close enough, I was surprised to see that her propellers were idle. She headed straight for that grim shaft. At the last minute, I saw the great propeller blades move to reverse her, yet on she came as though drawn by some mighty, irresistible power.

Intense excitement was evident on her deck, where men were running to man the guns and preparing to launch the small, one-man fliers.

The ship sped closer and closer to the black shaft. In another instant she would strike, and then I saw the signal that sends the smaller boats off from the deck of the mother ship.

Instantly, a hundred tiny fliers rose from her deck, like a swarm of huge dragon flies. They were barely clear of the battleship when the nose of each turned toward the shaft, and they, too, rushed toward the same inevitable end that menaced the larger vessel.

A moment later the collision came. The noise was deafening, and men were hurled in every direction from the ship's deck. The ship, bent and crumpled, took the long plunge to the scrap heap at the shaft's base. A shower of her tiny fliers fell with her, as each of them collided with the shaft. I noticed that the wrecked fliers scraped down the shaft's side and that their fall was not as rapid as might have been expected. It was then that the secret of the shaft came to me.

The shaft was an immense magnet! When a vessel came within its powerful attraction for the aluminum steel that is so largely utilized in the construction of all Barsoomian aircraft, nothing could prevent the result we just witnessed. I learned later that the shaft rests directly over the magnetic pole of Mars, but whether this adds in any way to its immense attraction power I do not know. I am a fighting man, not a scientist.

Here, at last, was an explanation of the long absence of Tardos Mors and Mors Kajak. These valiant warriors had dared the mysteries and dangers of the frozen north to search for Carthoris, whose long absence had caused such suffering to his beautiful mother, Dejah Thoris, Princess of Helium.

The moment that the last of the fliers came to rest at the base of the shaft the black-bearded, yellow warriors swarmed over the mass of wreckage. They made prisoners of those who were uninjured and killed the wounded. A few of the uninjured red men battled bravely against their cruel foes, but for the most part they seemed too overwhelmed by the horror of the catastrophe to do more than submit.

When the last of the prisoners had been confined, our hunting party returned to the city. At the entry gate, we met a pack of fierce, gold-collared apts. Two warriors held each of them controlled by chains as they marched them out of the gate.

Just beyond the gate the attendants set loose the whole terrible herd, and as they bounded off toward the grim, black shaft I realized their mission. If not for my plan to rescue the living, I would have risked much to do battle with these creatures on their way toward the dead red men out there tangled up in the broken wreckage of their aircraft. As it was, I could only follow the yellow warriors and give thanks for our easy entry into the capital of Salensus Oll. Once inside the gates, we had no difficulty in eluding our hunting friends and soon found ourselves in a Martian inn.

CHAPTER 10

In Durance

The inns of Barsoom are much the same as you go from place to place. There is no privacy other than for married couples. Men without their wives are taken to a large chamber. The floor is usually made of white marble or heavy glass and kept scrupulously clean. The room is crowded with many small, raised sleeping platforms.

Once a man's belongings have been deposited on one of these platforms, he is a guest of the house, and that platform belongs to him until he leaves. No one will disturb his belongings—there are no thieves on Mars.

Because assassination is the one thing to be feared, the owners furnish armed guards, who pace back and forth through the sleeping room day and night. The number of guards and their fancy trappings usually display the status of the hotel.

No meals are served in these houses, but generally a public eating place is close by. Baths are connected with the sleeping chambers, and each guest is required to bathe daily.

Usually on another floor, there is a smaller sleeping room for single women guests, but its appointments do not vary much from the chamber occupied by men. The male guards who watch the women remain in the corridor outside, while female slaves pace back and forth among the guests, ready to call the guards if necessary.

I was surprised to note that all the guards at our hotel were red men. I talked with one of them and learned that they were slaves purchased from the government. This man had been navy commander serving a great Martian nation. Fate had carried his flagship across the ice barrier, and the magnetic shaft had caused its destruction. For many tedious years, he had been a slave of the yellow men.

He told me that princes, jeds, and even jeddaks of the outer world were among the slaves who served the yellow race. When I asked him if he had heard of the fate of Mors Kajak or Tardos Mors, he shook his head, saying that he never had heard of their being prisoners here.

He also told me that he had heard nothing about the Father of Therns and Thurid the First Born, but he quickly explained that he knew little of what took place inside the palace. I could see that he wondered why a yellow man should be so interested in certain red prisoners from beyond the ice barrier.

In fact, I had forgotten my disguise when I saw a red man pacing next to my sleeping platform. His expression of surprise warned me in time—I did not want to reveal my identity to anyone unless some good could come of it. I did not see how this poor fellow could serve me yet, though I knew I might soon serve him and all the other thousands of prisoners who do the bidding of their yellow masters in Kadabra.

Thuvan Dihn and I discussed our plans that night in the midst of the hundreds of yellow men who occupied the room with us. We spoke in low whispers, but that is what courtesy demands in a public sleeping place, and we aroused no suspicion. At last, knowing that our talk was only idle speculation until after we explored the city, we turned to sleep.

After breakfast the following morning, we set out to see Kadabra. The prince of Marentina supplied us with plenty of funds, so we purchased a ground flier. We spent the day exploring the city, and late in the afternoon, we stopped at a magnificent building on the plaza opposite the royal grounds and the palace. We walked boldly past the armed guard at the door and were met by a red slave who asked our wishes.

"Tell Sorav, your master, that two warriors from Illall wish to take service in the palace guard," I said.

Talu had told us that Sorav was the commander of the forces of the palace. Men from the farther cities of Okar—and especially Illall—were less likely to be spies or assassins, so he was sure that we would be welcomed.

Talu had primed us with enough general information to pass muster with Sorav. After that, we would have to go through another examination by Salensus Oll, so he could determine our physical fitness and assess our fighting skills.

The little experience we had had with the strange hooked sword and cuplike shield of the yellow man made it unlikely that either of us could pass this final test. We were pleased that we would be quartered in the palace after being accepted by Sorav, and it might be some time before Salensus Oll would find time to test us. This would give us time to investigate the palace.

After a wait of several minutes, we were summoned into the private office of Sorav and were courteously greeted by this black-bearded officer. He asked us questions that Talu had prepared us for. The interview ended, and Sorav summoned an aid and had us escorted to the quarters reserved for the palace guard.

The aid first took us to his own office where he measured and weighed and photographed us with a machine ingeniously devised for that purpose, five copies being instantly reproduced in five different offices of the government. He then led us through the palace grounds to our quarters.

We were located on the second floor in a semi-detached tower. When we asked our guide why we were quartered so far from the guard-room, he said that the older members of the guard sometimes picked quarrels with recruits to test their skill. This had resulted in so many deaths that it was difficult to maintain the guard at its full strength. Salensus Oll had set these quarters apart for recruits, so they were safe from danger of attack.

This information put a sudden stop to our well-laid plans. It meant that we were virtually prisoners in the palace of Salensus Oll until he would give us our final examination. It was during this period that we hoped to do our search for Dejah Thoris and Thuvia. Our spirits sank when we heard the lock click behind our guide as he left us. I turned to Thuvan Dihn. He shook his head and walked to one of the windows on the far side of the apartment where he gave a gasp of surprise. "Look!" said Thuvan Dihn, pointing toward the courtyard below.

I saw two women pacing back and forth in an enclosed garden. I instantly recognized Dejah Thoris and Thuvia of Ptarth! I had trailed them from one Pole of this planet to another, the length of a world. Only ten feet of space and a few metal bars now separated us.

With a sound, I attracted their attention, and as Dejah Thoris looked up into my eyes, I made the sign of love that the men of Barsoom make to their women.

To my astonishment, her head went high, and a look of contempt touched her face as she turned her back to me. My body is covered with the scars of a thousand conflicts, but never in all my long life have I suffered such hurt from a wound, for this time the steel of a woman's look had entered my heart.

With a groan, I turned away and buried my face in my arms. I heard Thuvan Dihn call out to Thuvia, but an instant later, his surprise showed that he, too, had been repulsed. "They will not even listen!" he moaned. "They put their hands over their ears and walked to the far end of the garden. Have you ever seen anything like this, John Carter? The two must be bewitched!"

I got up enough courage to go back to the window . . . I still loved her, even if she rejected me. I could not keep my eyes off her, but when she saw me looking she turned away again. I was at my wit's end to account for her strange actions. The fact that Thuvia had also turned against her father seemed incredible.

Could it be that my princess still clung to that awful religion that I had destroyed? Could she hate me because I had returned from the Valley Dor and flaunted custom? Did she object to my invasion of the temples of the Holy Therns?

Any of these seemed impossible! The love of Dejah Thoris for John Carter had been a great and wondrous love—far above any creed or religion.

As I gazed at her, a gate opened, and a man entered. He appeared to slip money into the hand of the yellow guardsman. Instantly I knew that this newcomer had bribed his way inside the garden. Then as he turned toward the women, I saw that he was Thurid of the First Born!

He approached them, and they turned at the sound of his voice. I saw Dejah Thoris shrink away from him. He had a leer on his face as he stepped close and spoke again. I could not hear his words, but her answer came clearly. "The granddaughter of Tardos Mors can always die, but she could never live at the price you name," she said.

Then I saw the black scoundrel go down on his knees, pleading with her. I could only hear part of what he said. It was apparent that he did not want to raise his voice but I overheard, "I would save you from Matai Shang! You know the fate that awaits you at his hands. Choose between me and Matai Shang!"

"I would not choose either one!" snapped Dejah Thoris.

"No one can rescue you!" he cried. "John Carter, Prince of Helium, is dead."

"I know better than that! But even if he was dead, I would choose a plant man or a great white ape before either Matai Shang or you, black calot," she answered sharply.

All of a sudden, the beast lost control and grabbed her by the throat. Thuvia screamed and sprang to her aid, and at the same instant I, too, went mad. I tore at the bars that spanned my window and ripped them aside like they were copper wire.

I jumped through the window into the garden, but far from where Thurid was choking the life from my princess! With a single bound I reached them. I did not speak a word as I tore his fingers from her beautiful throat! I did not make a sound as I picked him up and threw him twenty feet. Foaming with rage, Thurid got to his feet and charged me like a mad bull.

"Yellow man," he shrieked, "you do not know who you have laid your hands on! Before I am done with you, you will know what it means to offend a First Born!"

Then he was on me, reaching for my throat, and just like I had done that day in the courtyard of the Temple of Issus, I did here in Salensus Oll's palace. I ducked under his outstretched arms, and as he lunged past me, I planted a terrific right punch on the side of his jaw.

Just as he had done on that other occasion, he did now. He spun around like a top, his knees gave way, and he crumpled to the ground out cold. Then I heard a voice behind me yell, "Cease!"

It was the deep voice of authority that marks the ruler of men. I turned to face a giant yellow man. I knew without asking that it was Salensus Oll. Matai Shang stood beside him, and a score of guardsmen followed behind.

"Who are you?" he cried. "What are you doing here inside the women's garden? I do not recall your face. How did you get in here?"

If not for his last words, I might have forgotten my disguise and told him that I was John Carter, Prince of Helium.

I pointed to the damaged bars of the window and said, "I am a palace guard recruit, and from yonder window I saw this brute attack this woman. I could not stand idly by and see this act done within your palace grounds! I would not feel that I was fit to serve and guard your royal person."

I made an impression on the ruler of Okar by my words. After he turned to Dejah Thoris and Thuvia of Ptarth, and both had corroborated my statements, it began to look pretty dark for Thurid.

I saw the ugly gleam in Matai Shang's eyes as Dejah Thoris told the jeddak all that had happened after Thurid entered the garden. When she came to the part about my interference with the brute, her gratitude was quite apparent, though I could see that something puzzled her. I understood her attitude toward me while others were present, but she had rejected me while she and Thuvia were alone, and this hurt me deeply.

As the examination proceeded, I cast a glance at Thurid as he woke up and caught him looking directly at me. Then, suddenly, he laughed in my face.

Salensus Oll turned toward the black and asked, "What do you have to say for yourself? Do you dare to want the woman who the Father of Therns has chosen—a woman who might even be a fit mate for the Jeddak of Jeddaks himself?"

And then the black-bearded tyrant turned with a greedy look at Dejah Thoris, as though with his words a new thought and a new desire had sprung up in his mind.

Thurid was about to reply, and a cunning look crept into his eyes. I knew from the expression on his face that his next words were not the ones he had intended to speak. He stammered out, "O Mightiest of Jeddaks, the man and the women do not speak the truth. This fellow came into the garden to help the two women escape. I was outside and overheard their conversation. When I entered the garden the woman screamed, and the man attacked and tried to kill me.

"What do you know about this man? He is a stranger to you, and I dare say that you will find him an enemy and a spy. Let him be put on trial, Salensus Oll, rather than your friend and guest, Thurid, Dator of the First Born."

Salensus Oll looked puzzled. He turned again and looked at Dejah Thoris, and then Thurid stepped close to him and whispered in his ear—what, I do not know. The jeddak turned to one of his officers, pointed at me, and commanded, "See that this man is securely confined until we have time to go deeper into this affair. Bars alone seem inadequate, so chain him to a wall!"

He left the garden, taking Dejah Thoris with him—his hand on her shoulder. Thurid and Matai Shang also went out, and as they reached the gateway, the black turned and laughed again.

What could be the meaning of his sudden change toward me? Could he suspect my true identity? I bet it was the boxing trick and punch that knocked him out for the second time.

As the guards dragged me away, my heart was bitter, for now I had to add someone else to my list of enemies. I would have been a fool to not recognize the evil heart of Salensus Oll, Jeddak of Jeddaks, ruler of Okar, and his desire for Dejah Thoris, my wife and princess.

CHAPTER
11

The Pit of Plenty

I did not stay long in prison. During the short time that I lay there, shackled with chains of gold, I wondered what happened to Thuvan Dihn, Jeddak of Ptarth.

My brave companion had followed me into the garden as I attacked Thurid. When Salensus Oll left with Dejah Thoris and the others, Thuvia stayed behind. Thuvan Dihn remained in the garden with his daughter, unnoticed—he was dressed similar to the guards. Could it be possible that they had escaped?

Three days later, a dozen warriors escorted me to Salensus Oll for trial. A great number of nobles crowded the room, and among them I saw Thurid, but Matai Shang was not there. Dejah Thoris, as radiantly beautiful as ever, sat on a small throne next to Salensus Oll. Her expression of sad hopelessness cut deep into my heart.

I knew her position beside the Jeddak of Jeddaks meant trouble for both of us. I also knew I would never leave that chamber alive if I had to leave her in the clutches of this powerful tyrant. I had killed better men than Salensus Oll with my bare hands. I knew it would mean almost instant death for me, but it would also unfortunately remove me from helping Dejah Thoris. For this reason, I decided to wait for the outcome of the trial so I would learn all that I could of the ruler's intentions and then act accordingly.

Salensus Oll immediately summoned Thurid. "Dator Thurid," he said, "you have made an unusual request, but I will allow it."

"You tell me that a certain announcement will result in convicting this prisoner and, at the same time, grant me my dearest wish."

Thurid nodded.

"Then shall I make the announcement at this time," continued Salensus Oll. "For a year no queen has sat on the throne beside me, and now it suits me to take as wife one who is said to be the most beautiful woman on Barsoom.

"Nobles of Okar, unsheathe your swords and do homage to Dejah Thoris, Princess of Helium and future Queen of Okar, for in ten days she shall become the wife of Salensus Oll."

The nobles drew their blades and lifted them high, in accordance with the ancient custom of Okar when a jeddak announces his intention to wed. Dejah Thoris sprang to her feet and cried in a loud voice that they desist.

"I can not become the wife of Salensus Oll," she pleaded, "for I am already a wife and mother. John Carter, Prince of Helium, still lives! I know it to be true, for I overheard Matai Shang tell his daughter Phaidor that he had seen him in Kaor. A jeddak does not wed a married woman! Salensus Oll must not violate the bonds of matrimony!"

Salensus Oll turned on Thurid with an ugly look and demanded, "Is this the surprise you held for me? You assured me that no obstacle stood between me and this woman, and now I find that one insurmountable obstacle stops me. What have you to say?"

"If I deliver John Carter into your hands, Salensus Oll, would you feel I satisfied the promise that I made you?" answered Thurid.

"Do not talk like a fool!" yelled the enraged jeddak. "I am no child to be played with!"

"I am talking only as a man who knows that he can do all that he claims," was Thurid's quick reply.

"Then turn John Carter over to me within ten days, or you will die like he would die if he were in my power!" snapped the Jeddak of Jeddaks, with an ugly scowl.

"You need not wait ten days, Salensus Oll," replied Thurid. He turned toward me, extended his arm, pointed an accusing finger at me and cried, "There stands John Carter, Prince of Helium!"

"Fool!" shrieked Salensus Oll. "Fool! John Carter is a white man. This fellow is as yellow as I am. John Carter's face is smooth—Matai Shang has described him to me. This prisoner has a beard and mustache as large and black as any in Okar. Quick, guardsmen! To the pits with the black maniac who wishes to throw his life away for a poor joke!"

"Hold on!" cried Thurid, and springing forward before I could guess his intention, he had grabbed my beard and ripped the whole false disguise from my face and head, revealing my smooth, tanned skin and my close-cropped black hair!

Instantly, pandemonium swept the room! Warriors pressed forward with drawn blades, thinking that I might be contemplating the assassination of the Jeddak of Jeddaks. Others, out of curiosity to see someone whose name was famous from Pole to Pole, crowded in behind.

As my identity was revealed, I saw Dejah Thoris spring to her feet and stare in amazement. Then she forced her way through the armed men before anyone could stop her. In only a moment she was in front of me with outstretched arms and eyes filled with the light of her love.

"John Carter! John Carter!" she cried as I held her close, and then I realized why she had rejected me in the garden. What a fool I had been! To expect she could penetrate the disguise that had been given to me by the barber of Marentina! She had not recognized me—that was all. When she saw the sign of love from a stranger she was offended and indignant. I was a fool.

"It was you," she cried, "who spoke to me from the tower! How could I dream that my beloved Virginian was behind that fierce beard and that yellow skin?"

She had been calling me her Virginian as a term of endearment. She knew that I loved the sound of that beautiful name, made a thousand times more beautiful by her lovely lips. As I heard it again, my eyes dimmed with tears and my voice choked with emotion.

But I was only able to hold her for an instant before Salensus Oll, trembling with rage and jealousy, shouldered his way to us and commanded, "Seize this man, and take him away!" and a hundred ruthless hands tore us apart.

It was good for the nobles of the court of Okar that I had been disarmed. As it was, a dozen of them felt the weight of my clenched fists. I fought my way almost to the throne where Salensus Oll had dragged Dejah Thoris before they could stop me.

I went down beneath fifty warriors. Before they had battered me to unconsciousness, I heard Dejah Thoris shouting to the jeddak and all his men, "Salensus Oll! Even if he were a thousand times dead, do you think that the wife of a man like that would ever dishonor his memory by mating with a lesser mortal? Is there anyone else alive on any world like John Carter, Prince of Helium? Lives there another man who could fight his way back and forth across a warlike planet, facing savage beasts and hordes of savage men, for the love of a woman?

"I, Dejah Thoris, Princess of Helium, am his. He fought for me and won me. If you think you are a brave man, you will honor his bravery, and you will not kill him. Make him a slave if you will, but spare his life! I would rather be a slave with him than be Queen of Okar!"

"Neither slave nor queen dictates to Salensus Oll," replied the Jeddak of Jeddaks. "John Carter shall die a natural death in the Pit of Plenty, and the day he dies Dejah Thoris will become my queen."

I did not hear her reply as I was battered unconscious. When I recovered my senses, only a handful of guardsmen remained in the audience chamber with me. As I opened my eyes, they forced me up and led me away to the Pit of Plenty.

We eventually reached it and found a half a dozen other guardsmen standing at its edge, awaiting me. One of them carried a long rope in his hands. We got to within fifty feet of these men when I felt a sudden strange and rapid pricking sensation in one of my fingers. It took a moment for me to remember the gift ring of Prince Talu of Marentina.

Instantly, I looked toward the group we were nearing, at the same time raising my left hand to my forehead so the ring would be visible. Simultaneously, one of the waiting warriors raised his left hand to brush back his hair, and I saw the duplicate of my own ring.

A quick look passed between us, but afterward, I kept my eyes turned away and did not look at him again. When we reached the edge of the pit, I saw that it was very deep. The man who held the rope passed it around my body in such a way that it could be released from above. The group then threw me over the edge into the abyss.

They lowered me quickly but smoothly. The moment before the plunge, while two or three of the men had been assisting in adjusting the rope, one of them breathed a single word into my ear: "Courage!"

The pit, which my imagination had pictured as bottomless, proved to be about a hundred feet deep. Its walls were so smoothly polished that it might as well have been a thousand feet—I could never escape without assistance.

I was left in darkness for an entire day, and then, quite suddenly, a brilliant light lit up my prison. I was hungry and thirsty by this time—I had not had a drink or tasted food since the day before.

To my amazement, I found the sides of the pit, that I had thought smooth, lined with shelves holding delicious foods and liquid refreshments.

With an exclamation of delight, I sprang toward the food, but before I reached it the light was extinguished. Though I groped my way all around the chamber, my hands felt nothing except the smooth, hard wall that I had seen on my first examination.

Where, before, I had only a mild craving for food and drink, I now actually suffered, and all because of the tantalizing sight of that food almost within my grasp. Once more, darkness and silence enveloped me, a silence that was broken only by a single mocking laugh.

For another day, nothing occurred to break the monotony of my imprisonment or relieve my suffering. Slowly the hunger pangs became less sharp, as suffering deadened the activity of certain nerves. Then the light flashed on again, and I saw an array of new and tempting dishes, with bottles of clear water and jugs of wine.

Again, with the hungry madness of a wild beast, I sprang toward those tempting dishes; but, like before, the light went out, and I came to a sudden stop against a hard wall. Then the mocking laugh rang out for a second time.

The Pit of Plenty!

Ah, what a cruel mind must have devised this torture! Day after day the cycle repeated until I was on the verge of madness. Then, as I had done in the pits of the Warhoons, I took a new, firm hold on my reason and forced it back into the channels of sanity.

By sheer willpower, I got control of my tottering mentality, and the next time that the light came on I sat quite still and looked indifferently at the fresh and tempting food. It was good that I did this for it gave me an opportunity to solve the mystery of those vanishing banquets.

Since I made no move to reach the food, the torturers left the light turned on in the hope that I would react. As I sat looking at the shelves, I saw how the trick was done. It was so simple, I wondered why I had not figured it out before. The wall of my prison was of clearest glass— behind the glass was the tantalizing food.

After nearly an hour the light went out, but this time there was no mocking laughter—at least not on the part of my tormentors. I, however, gave a low laugh that no one could mistake for a maniac.

Nine days passed, and I was weak from hunger and thirst, but no longer suffering—I was beyond that. Then, down through the darkness above, a little parcel fell to the floor at my side. Indifferently, I groped for it, thinking it was some new invention of my jailers to add to my suffering.

At last I found it—a tiny package wrapped in paper, at the end of a strong and slender cord. As I opened it, a few lozenges fell to the floor. As I gathered them up, I discovered that they were tablets of concentrated food quite common in all parts of Barsoom.

Poison! I thought.

Well, what of it? Why not end my misery now rather than drag out a few more wretched days in this dark pit? Slowly I raised one of the little pellets to my lips as I whispered, "Goodbye, my Dejah Thoris! I have lived for you and fought for you, and now my next dearest wish is to be realized, for I shall die for you," and I choked down the first little pellet.

One by one, I ate them all. Never did anything taste better than those tiny bits of nourishment. I was afraid they might contain the seeds of death—possibly of some hideous, torturing death.

As I sat quietly on the floor of my prison, waiting for the end, my fingers by accident came in contact with the bit of paper in which the things had been wrapped. As I idly played with it,

I became aware of strange bumps on the smooth surface of the parchment-like substance. I was mildly curious what they were. After a while they seemed to take form, and then I realized they were like writing.

My fingers traced and retraced the mysterious bumps. There were four separate and distinct combinations of raised lines. These were four words, and they carried a message for me! The more I thought about it the more excited I became. My fingers raced back and forth over those little hills and valleys on that scrap of paper.

I could make out nothing, and at last I decided to take it more slowly. Again and again I traced the first of those four combinations. They baffled me for some time, but at last I made out the first word. It was "courage."

Courage!

That was the word the yellow guardsman had whispered in my ear as I stood at the edge of the Pit of Plenty. The message must be from him, and I knew he was a friend. With renewed hope, I deciphered the rest of the message, and at last I read the four words: "Courage! Follow the rope."

"FOLLOW THE ROPE."

What could it mean?

"Follow the rope." What rope?

I recalled the cord attached to the parcel when it fell, and after a little groping, I found it again. It came down from above, and when I pulled it, I discovered that it was securely attached to something solid.

The cord, though thin, seemed very strong. I then made another discovery—there was a second message tied in the rope. This one I figured out more easily. "Bring the rope with you. Beyond the knots lies danger."

I was not sure of the meaning of: "Beyond the knots lies danger," but I knew this was an avenue of escape! The sooner I took advantage of it, the better.

I had climbed up some fifty feet when a noise above attracted my attention. I saw that the covering of the pit was being removed, and in the light of the courtyard, I saw a number of yellow warriors.

Could it be that I was laboriously working my way into some new trap? Were the messages a trap? And then I saw two things.

One was the body of a huge, struggling, snarling apt being lowered over the side of the pit, and the other was an opening in the side of the shaft!

Just as I scrambled into the hole, the apt passed me, reaching out with his claws and snapping, growling, and roaring in a most frightful manner.

Salensus Oll had starved me, and now he had

this fierce beast lowered into my prison to finish the job.

Another truth came to me—I had lived nine days of the ten that must pass before Salensus Oll could make Dejah Thoris his queen. The purpose of the apt was to insure my death before the tenth day.

Coiling up the rope that had carried me so far on my strange journey, I searched for the other end, but found that it went on into the distance. So this was the meaning of the words: "Follow the rope."

I crawled through a tunnel that was low and dark. I followed it for a while until I felt a knot and remembered: "Beyond the knots lies danger." A couple of sharp turns in the tunnel brought me to an opening into a large, bright chamber.

I saw many strange instruments and devices along the walls and, in the center of the room, two men in earnest conversation. The one who faced me was a yellow man—a little, pasty-faced old fellow with big eyes. His companion was a black man, and I did not need to see his face to know that it was Thurid.

Thurid was speaking as I poked my head around a corner, "Solan, there is no risk, and the reward is great. You know that you hate Salensus Oll and that nothing would please you more than to thwart him in some cherished plan. There is nothing that he cherishes more today than wedding the beautiful Princess of Helium; but I, too, want her, and with your help I may win her.

"You only have to leave this room for an instant when I give you the signal. I will do the rest, and then, when I am gone, you may come and throw the switch back to its place, and all will be as before. I need only an hour's start to be safe away from the devilish power that you control. See how easy," and with the words the black dator got up from his seat and laid his hand on a large, burnished lever.

"No! No!" cried the little old man, springing after him. "Not that one! Not that one! That controls the sunray tanks, and if you pull it too far down, all Kadabra would be consumed by heat. Get away! Get away from there! You do not know about the powers controlled here! This is the lever that you seek. Remember the symbol on its surface."

Thurid approached and examined the lever. "Ah, the symbol for a magnet," he said. "I will remember."

The old man hesitated. A look of greed and apprehension spread over his features. "Double the figure," he said. "Even that amount will be too small for the service you ask. Why, I risk my life by even allowing you here inside my station.

If Salensus Oll learned about this, he would have me thrown to the apts."

"He would not dare to do that, and you know it, Solan," contradicted the black. "You hold the power of life and death over the people of Kadabra. Salensus Oll would never risk threatening you with death. Before his warriors could lay their hands on you, you could seize this lever and wipe out the entire city."

"And myself into the bargain," said Solan, with a shudder.

"But if you were to die anyway, you would find the nerve to do it," replied Thurid.

"Yes," muttered Solan, "I have often thought about that very thing. Well, First Born, is your red princess worth the price I ask for my services, or will you go without her and see her in the arms of Salensus Oll tomorrow night?"

"Take your price, yellow man," replied Thurid. "Half now and the balance when you have fulfilled your contract."

With that the dator threw a well-filled money pouch at the yellow man's feet. Solan opened the pouch and with trembling fingers counted its contents. Having satisfied himself that the amount was correct, he said, "Now, are you quite sure that you know the way to your destination? You must travel quickly to cover the ground to the cave, and from there to the Great Power

Shaft, all within an hour. I can spare you no more time than that!"

"Let me repeat it to you," said Thurid, "so you can see that I am letter-perfect."

"Go through that door, follow the corridor, passing three side corridors on the right; then go into the fourth right-hand corridor to where three corridors meet; take the one on the right, hugging the wall to avoid a pit trap. At the end go down a spiral runway; after that follow the tunnel to the exit.

"Am I right?"

"Quite right, Dator," answered Solan; "and now go! You have already tempted fate too long inside this forbidden place."

"Tonight, or tomorrow, you may expect the signal," said Thurid, rising to go.

"Tonight or tomorrow," repeated Solan, and as the door closed he turned back to the table, where he dumped out the contents of the money pouch. He stayed there, running his fingers through the heap of shining metal; piling the coins into little towers; counting, recounting, and fondling the wealth as he muttered on and on in a crooning undertone.

After a while his fingers ceased their play. His eyes popped wider than ever as they stared at the door through which Thurid had disappeared. The croon changed to muttering and finally to an ugly growl. Then the old man got up and started shaking his fist at the closed door. Now he raised his voice, and I heard his words distinctly, "Fool! Do you think that Solan will give up his life for your happiness? If you escaped, Salensus Oll would know that I helped you. Then he would send for me. What would you have me do? Reduce the city and myself to ashes? No, fool, there is a better way—a better way for Solan to keep your money and get revenge on Salensus Oll."

He laughed in a nasty, cackling note.

"Poor fool! You may throw the great switch that will give you the freedom of the air of Okar, and then, in false security, go on with your red princess to the freedom of . . . death! When you have passed beyond this chamber in your flight, what can prevent me from replacing the switch as it was before your vile hand touched it? Nothing! Then the Guardian of the North will claim you and your woman! Salensus Oll, when he sees your dead bodies, will never dream that the hand of Solan had anything to do with your actions."

I thanked the luck that had led me to this chamber at such an important time, a time so important to Dejah Thoris and myself. But how do I get past the old man now? The cord, almost invisible on the floor, stretched straight across the room to a door on the far side. There was no other way! I must cross this room, but how could

I do it with that old man in the way?

Of course I could dash in and strangle him and silence him forever, but I had heard enough to make me think that with him alive he might serve me at some future moment. If I killed him and someone else was stationed here, Thurid's plan with Dejah Thoris would change to something I did not know about.

I watched the old man as he carried the money pouch to one end of the room, where he fumbled with a panel in the wall. I guessed that he was opening the hiding place where he hoarded his wealth. While his back was toward me, I entered the chamber and crept to the opposite side before he finished what he was doing. He did not turn around, and I went out and gently closed the door.

I made my way along the new corridor, following the rope, which I coiled and brought with me as I advanced. Only a short distance farther on, I came to the rope's end at a point where five corridors met. What was I to do? Which way should I turn?

An examination of the end of the rope showed that it had been cleanly cut. This fact and the words that had warned me that danger lay beyond the KNOTS convinced me that the rope had been severed sometime after my friend had placed it as my guide. I knew I had only passed a single knot, so there had been two or more along the length of the cord.

Now, I knew I was in trouble. I did not know which corridor to follow, and I wouldn't be warned of future dangers on the path. I chose the central opening and passed into its gloomy depths. The floor of the tunnel rose rapidly, and a moment later the path came to an abrupt end at a heavy door. I could hear nothing on the other side. I pushed it open and stepped into a room filled with yellow warriors.

The first to see me opened his eyes wide in astonishment, and at the same instant, I felt the tingling sensation in my finger that warned me of the presence of a friend of the ring. Then others saw me, and they rushed over to capture me, for these were all members of the palace guard—men familiar with my face.

The first to reach me was the wearer of the mate to my strange ring, and as he came close he whispered: "Surrender to me!" then in a loud voice shouted: "You are my prisoner, white man," and menaced me with his two weapons. And so I meekly surrendered. The other guardsmen now swarmed around us, and finally my captor announced that he would lead me back to my prison.

An officer ordered several other warriors to go with us, and a moment later we were retracing the way I had just come. My friend walked close beside me, asking many silly questions about my life in Helium and the battles I had fought, until finally the other men paid no further attention to him.

Gradually, as he spoke, he lowered his voice, so that he was able to converse with me in a low tone without attracting attention. His ruse was a clever one and showed that Talu knew the man's fitness for dangerous duty.

He asked me why I had not followed the rope. When I told him that I had reached its end at the five corridors he said that it must have been cut by someone in need of a piece of rope, for he was sure that "the stupid Kadabrans would never have guessed its purpose."

As we came to a sharp corner right before we reached the spot where the five corridors came together, my Marentinian friend whispered: "Run up the first corridor on the right. It leads to the watchtower on the south wall. I will direct the pursuit up the next corridor," and as we turned the corner he shoved me forward at the same time crying out in pain and alarm as he threw himself on the floor like I had knocked him down.

I ran for my life through the dark galleries beneath the palace of Salensus Oll. I ran, but my face showed a broad grin as I thought of the resourcefulness of the nameless hero of Marentina. The corridor stopped at the foot of a spiral runway, and I went up to a circular chamber on the first floor of a tower.

I saw a dozen red slaves polishing or repairing the weapons of the yellow men. The walls of the room were lined with racks holding hundreds of straight and hooked swords, javelins, and daggers. There were only four yellow warriors guarding the workers.

My eyes took in the entire scene at a glance. Here were plenty of weapons and the red warriors to wield them! And here was John Carter, Prince of Helium, in need both of weapons and warriors!

As I stepped into the room, both guards and prisoners saw me at the same time. There was a rack of straight swords close to the entrance, and as I grabbed one I recognized two of the prisoners.

One of the guards started toward me. "Who are you?" he demanded. "What are you doing here?"

"I come for Tardos Mors, Jeddak of Helium and his son, Mors Kajak!" I shouted, pointing to the two red prisoners as they jumped to their feet, wide-eyed in astonishment.

"Rise, red men! Before we die let us leave a memorial in the palace of Okar's tyrant that will stand forever to the honor and glory of Helium!"

Then the first guardsman engaged me, and the fight was on. As my sword slashed into this man, and he collapsed screaming, I turned and noticed that all the red slaves were shackled to the floor and unable to come to my aid!

CHAPTER

The Magnet Switch

The guardsmen paid no attention to the slaves. The red men could not move more that two feet from where they were locked, though each had seized a weapon. The three yellow men gave all their attention to me. I wished that I had had my own sword in my hand that day; but I gave a decent account of myself with the unfamiliar weapon.

At first it was difficult dodging their villainous hook-swords, but after a minute or two, I grabbed a second sword from the racks along the wall. After that I felt better equipped to handle this type of fighting. They were attacking me like madmen, and except for a lucky circumstance, my end might have come quickly. One guardsman made a vicious lunge with his hook after they had backed me against the wall, but as I sidestepped and raised my arm, his weapon grazed my side and got stuck in a rack of javelins.

Before he could release it, I had run him through, and then, falling back upon the tactics that have saved me a hundred times in tight pinches, I rushed the remaining warriors. I forced them back with a torrent of cuts and thrusts, weaving my sword in and out until I had the fear of death in them.

Then one of them tried to call for help, but it was too late to save these unlucky fools. They were putty in my hands now, and I backed them around the armory until I had them where I wanted them—within reach of the shackled slaves. In an instant both lay dead on the floor. But those cries for help were successful, for I heard shouts and the sounds of many men running.

"The door! Quick, John Carter, bar the door!" cried Tardos Mors.

The troops were already in sight, charging across the open court that was visible through the doorway. In seconds they would be in the tower. A single leap carried me to the heavy door. With a resounding bang, I slammed it shut.

"The bar!" shouted Tardos Mors.

I tried to slip the huge piece of wood into place, but I could not get it placed correctly! I could hear the yellow warriors just beyond the door. I raised the bar and shot it to the right just as the first of the guardsmen threw himself against the massive panels. The barrier held—I had been in time, but only by a fraction of a second.

Now I turned my attention to the prisoners. I yelled to Tardos Mors first and asked him where the keys would be.

"The officer of the guard has them, and he is outside trying to get in!" was the hurried reply.

Most of the prisoners were already hacking at their bonds with the swords in their hands. The yellow men were battering at the door with javelins and axes. I turned my attention to the chains that held Tardos Mors. Again and again I cut deep into the chain with my sharp blade, but faster and louder came the torrent of blows on the door. At last a link of the chain came apart and a moment later Tardos Mors was free, though a few inches of trailing chain still dangled from his ankle.

A hunk of wood was hacked out of the door and announced the headway that our enemies were making in toward us. The mighty panels trembled and bent beneath the furious onslaught of the enraged yellow men.

What with the battering on the door and the red men chopping at their chains, the din inside the armory was appalling. Tardos Mors cut himself free and immediately turned his attention to help another of the prisoners, while I tried to liberate Mors Kajak. We had to work fast if we were going to release all these men before the door gave way! Now a panel crashed inward, and Mors Kajak sprang to defend the opening until we had time to release the others.

He snatched a few javelins from the wall, threw them through the hole in the door, and killed several Okarians while we battled with the chains that stood between our friends and freedom. All but one of the prisoners got loose before the door fell in with a crash, and the yellow horde was upon us.

"To the upper chambers!" shouted the red man who was still chained to the floor. "To the upper chambers! You can defend the tower against all Kadabra. Do not stop for me! I pray for no better death than in the service of Tardos Mors and the Prince of Helium!"

"Cut his chains!" I cried to two of the red men. "The rest of us can hold off these devils!"

There were ten of us now to do battle with the Okarian guard, and that ancient watchtower never looked down on a more hotly contested battle than took place that day. The first wave of yellow warriors recoiled from the slashing blades of ten of Helium's veteran fighting men. A dozen Okarian corpses blocked the doorway, but a wave of them charged over that barrier shouting their war-cry.

We met them on the bloody mound, hand to hand, stabbing where the quarters were too close to cut, and swinging our swords when we could push an enemy to arm's length. Mingled with the wild sounds of the Okarian dying and wounded was our war-cry, "For Helium! For Helium!"

We finally cut the chains off the last red man, and thirteen of us now met each new charge of our enemy. All of us were bleeding from wounds, but no one had fallen. We saw hundreds of guardsmen outside in the courtyard, and along the lower corridor from where I had entered, we could hear the clank of metal and the shouts of many more men.

In a moment we would be attacked from two sides, and even with all our fighting ability, we could not withstand these odds. Tardos Mors shouted, "To the upper chambers!" and a moment later we fell back toward the ramp that led to the floors above.

We waged another battle here as we retreated from the doorway. Here we lost our first man, a fierce fellow we could not spare; but finally everyone had backed onto the ramp except me. I remained to hold back the Okarians until the others were safe above. In the mouth of the narrow ramp, only a single warrior could attack me at a time, so I had little difficulty stopping the enemy as the red men went up the ramp. Then, backing up slowly and fighting all the way, I started my ascent.

All the long way to the top of the tower, the guardsmen attacked me continuously. When one went down, another scrambled over the dead man to take his place. Finally, I came to the spacious glass-walled watchtower of Kadabra. Here my companions clustered ready to take my place, and for a moment's rest, I stepped to one side while they held the enemy off.

From the lofty perch I could see for miles in every direction. Toward the south stretched the rugged, ice-clad waste to the edge of the barrier. Toward the east and west and dimly toward the north, I could see other Okarian cities, while in the immediate foreground, just beyond the walls of Kadabra, the grim guardian shaft was plainly visible.

Then I looked down to the streets of Kadabra where I heard loud noises and saw a battle raging. I looked again beyond the city's walls and now saw armed men marching in long columns toward a nearby gate. I pressed against the glass wall of the observatory, not believing my eyes. With a shout of joy that was strange in the midst of the cursing and groaning of the battling men at the entrance to the chamber, I called to Tardos Mors.

As he joined me, I pointed down into the

streets of Kadabra and to the advancing columns. It was then that we both spotted the flags and banners of Helium! An instant later, every red man in the lofty chamber had seen the inspiring sight, and a shout of thanksgiving rang out that echoed through that age-old pile of stone. But still we had to fight on, for though our troops had entered Kadabra, the city was far from giving up, and the palace had not yet been assaulted.

Our troops below rushed the palace gate! Battering-rams smashed against its surface. Our troops were driven back by a deadly shower of javelins from the wall's top! Once again they charged, but an attack by a large force of Okarians from an intersecting avenue crumpled the head of the column, and the men of Helium went down beneath an overwhelming force.

The palace gate opened, and a force of the jeddak's own guard, picked men from the flower of the Okarian army, went out to shatter the broken regiments. For a moment, it looked as though nothing could stop the defeat, and then I saw a noble figure on a thoat—not the tiny thoat of the red man, but one of his huge cousins from the dead sea bottoms.

The awesome warrior forced his way to the front line, while the previously disorganized soldiers of Helium charged behind him. As he raised his head to challenge the men on the palace walls,

I saw his face, and my heart swelled in pride and happiness as the red warriors swarmed around their leader hacking the enemy to pieces. They won back the ground that they had just lost—and the face of the one on the mighty thoat was the face of my son—Carthoris of Helium.

A huge Martian war hound fought at his side, and I did not need a second look to know that it was Woola—my faithful Woola who had performed his task and brought the legions of Helium in the nick of time. I sighed as I thought that I might not be alive to witness it. The red men had not yet forced their way into the palace, but they were fighting well against the best that Okar afforded—valiant warriors who contested every inch of the way.

Now my attention was caught by a new element outside the city wall—a large body of mounted warriors towering above the red men. They were the huge green allies of Helium—the savage hordes from the dead sea bottoms of the far south.

In grim and terrible silence they rode on toward the gate, the padded hoofs of their frightful mounts giving forth no sound. They charged into the doomed city, and as they wheeled across the wide plaza in front of the palace of the Jeddak of Jeddaks, I saw, riding at their head, their mighty leader—Tars Tarkas, Jeddak of Thark.

My wish was granted—I saw my old friend battling once again, and though I was not battling shoulder to shoulder with him, I, too, would be fighting in the same cause here in the high tower of Okar.

It seemed that our foes would never cease their stubborn attacks, for still they came, though the way to our chamber was clogged with the bodies of their dead. At times they would pause long enough to drag back the corpses, and then fresh warriors would forge upward to taste the cup of death.

I had been taking my turn with the others in defending the approach to our retreat when Mors Kajak, who had been watching the battle in the street below, called me to his side. As I reached him, he pointed out across the waste of snow and ice toward the southern horizon. "Oh, no!" he cried, "those fliers are heading to a disaster, and there is no way we can warn them!"

As I looked I saw an immense fleet of aircraft approaching Kadabra from the direction of the ice barrier. On and on they came at a faster and faster rate of speed.

"The grim shaft that they call the Guardian of the North is overpowering them," said Mors Kajak sadly, "just as it attracted my fleet! See where my ships lie at the bottom of that shaft, crumpled and broken, a terrible monument to the force of destruction which no power can resist."

I, too, looked at the horrible graveyard, but there was something else I saw that Mors Kajak did not. In my mind's eye I saw a chamber filled with strange instruments, devices, and controls. In the center of the room was a little, pop-eyed old man counting his money. Most important of all, I saw a large switch with a small magnet inlaid on its black handle.

I glanced back at the fast-approaching fleet. In five minutes that mighty armada of the skies would be bent and worthless scrap, lying at the base of the shaft outside the city's wall. Yellow hordes would pour out from the gates to attack the few survivors stumbling blindly through the mass of wreckage. Then they would let loose the apts. I shuddered at the thought, for I vividly remembered the whole horrible scene.

I have always been quick to decide and act. The impulse that moves me, and then the doing of a deed, seem simultaneous. If my mind goes through the tedious formality of reasoning, it must be a subconscious act of which I am not aware. I have often won success while another man might still be at the endless task of comparing various alternatives.

And now clarity of action was key to the success of the thing that I had decided. Grasping my sword more firmly in my hand, I called to the red man at the opening to the runway to stand aside. "Make way for the Prince of Helium!" I shouted, and before the astonished yellow man who was fighting at the end of the line could gather his wits, my sword sliced clean through his neck, and I was rushing like a mad bull down on those behind him.

"Make way for the Prince of Helium!" I shouted as I cut a path through the terrified guardsmen of Salensus Oll. Hewing right and left, I beat my way down that warrior-choked ramp until, near the bottom, those below, thinking that an entire army was attacking, turned and fled.

The armory at the first floor was vacant when I entered. The last of the Okarians had fled out into the courtyard, so no one saw me go down the spiral stairway to the corridor below. Here I ran as rapidly as I could to the junction of the five corridors and plunged into the passageway that led to the control room of the old miser.

I burst into the room! The old man was sitting at a rickety table, but as he saw me he leaped to his feet, drawing his sword. With hardly a glance toward him I ran to the switch, but quick as I was, that wiry old fellow was there before me. He turned on me like a tiger, and I soon realized why Solan had been chosen for this important duty.

Never in all my life have I seen such won-drous swordsmanship and such uncanny agility as that ancient bag of bones displayed. He was in forty places at the same time, and before I real-ized the danger I was in, he almost made a mon-key of me—and a dead monkey at that.

It is strange how new and unexpected condi-tions bring out our unknown ability to meet them. That day in the buried chamber beneath the palace of Salensus Oll, I learned what swords-manship meant. I learned what heights of sword mastery I could attain when pitted against such a wizard of the blade as Solan.

For a time it seemed like he might beat me; but at last the skills lying dormant in me came out, and I fought as I had never dreamed a human being could fight. That the duel of a life-time took place in the dark recesses of a cellar, without a single appreciative eye as witness seemed to be almost a world calamity! Think about it! On Barsoom, where bloody strife is the first and greatest consideration of individuals, nations, and races, no one but the combatants watched the show!

I was fighting to reach the switch, and Solan was fighting to stop me. Though we stood three feet from the lever, I could not gain an inch toward it! I knew I had to reset it in time to save the oncoming fleet, and it must be done in the next few seconds. I tried my old rushing tactics, but I might as well have rushed a brick wall. But right was on my side, and I think that gives a man greater confidence than if he is battling for a wicked cause.

I knew I did not lack in confidence! I rushed Solan the next time on his right side and hoped that he would turn to meet my new line of attack, and turn he did! Now we fought with our sides toward the coveted goal—the switch was within reach of my right hand.

To drop my guard for an instant would risk death, but I saw no other way to rescue that oncoming fleet! As Solan made a wicked direct attack, I reached out my sword and caught the switch a sudden flick that moved it to its other setting.

Solan was so surprised that he forgot to finish his attack. He wheeled toward the switch with a loud shriek—his last shriek—for before his hand could touch the lever, my sword cut his heart in two.

CHAPTER 13

The Tide of Battle

Solan's last loud cry caught someone's attention, and a moment later, a dozen guardsmen burst into the chamber. I demolished the switch so it could not be used to turn on the magnet again, but the sudden appearance of these new warriors forced me to run out the first passageway I could find. They must have guessed which way I went, for I had gone only a short distance when I heard the sound of pursuit.

I did not want to stop and fight these men here when there was plenty of fighting elsewhere in the city—fighting that could be much more valuable to me and mine. But the fellows were gaining on me, and I did not know which way to go in this unfamiliar passageway. I realized that they would soon catch up unless I found a place to hide.

The corridor had risen rapidly since leaving Solan's room and now ran level, straight into the distance as far as I could see. If I went that way I would be in plain sight with no chance to escape. I saw a series of doors opening on either side of the corridor, I tried the first one that I reached. It was a small chamber, luxuriously furnished and led to some office or audience chamber.

A curtained doorway was on the far side of the room, and I heard the hum of voices from that direction. I quickly crossed the small chamber and looked inside. I saw perhaps fifty richly clad nobles of the court, standing in front of Salensus Oll, who was sitting on a throne.

"The hour has come," he was saying as I entered the apartment; "and though the enemies of Okar are within her gates, nothing will change the will of Salensus Oll. The lavish ceremony will be postponed so all warriors except you nobles can man their posts. You are the fifty that custom demands must witness the creation of a new queen in Okar.

"In a moment the ceremony will be completed, and we will return to the battle. The ex-Princess of Helium will look down from the queen's tower on the annihilation of her former countrymen and witnesses the greatness of her husband's warriors."

Turning to a courtier, he issued some command in a low voice. The man went to a small door and, swinging it wide, cried: "Make way for Dejah Thoris, future Queen of Okar!"

Two guardsmen appeared dragging the unwilling bride toward an altar I had not seen before. Her hands were still manacled behind her to prevent suicide. Her disheveled hair and panting breath showed that, even chained up, she had fought against this evil ceremony.

As he saw her enter the room, Salensus Oll got up and drew his sword, and then each of the fifty nobles drew their swords and raised them high. They formed an arch, and the poor, beautiful creature was dragged under it toward her doom.

My lips formed a grim smile as I thought of the rude awakening that lay in store for the ruler of Okar. My itching fingers fondled the hilt of my bloody sword. I watched as the procession moved slowly toward the throne. It consisted of a few priests who followed Dejah Thoris and the two guardsmen.

Suddenly I caught a fleeting glimpse of a black face peering from behind the draperies that covered the wall behind Salensus Oll. But my gaze shifted to the guardsmen as they forced the Princess of Helium up the steps to the side of the tyrant of Okar, and I had no eyes and no thoughts for anything else. A priest opened a book and, raising his hand, commenced to drone out a sing-song ritual. Salensus Oll reached for the hand of his bride.

I had intended to wait until a break in the action would give me some hope of success before I attacked. I knew that even though the entire ceremony might be completed, there would be no valid marriage while I lived. What I was most concerned about, of course, was the rescuing of Dejah Thoris—I wanted to take her away from this place! If I could do that before or after the mock marriage was a matter of secondary importance.

But when I saw the vile hand of Salensus Oll reach out for the hand of my beloved princess, I could not restrain myself! Before the nobles of Okar knew that anything had happened, I had leaped through their thin line and was up on the dais beside Dejah Thoris and Salensus Oll.

With the flat of my sword, I struck down his polluting hand, and grabbing Dejah Thoris, I swung her behind me. With my back against the draperies, I faced the tyrant of the North and his roomful of noble warriors.

The Jeddak of Jeddaks was a mountain of a man—a coarse, brutal beast of a man! As he towered above me, his fierce black whiskers and mustache bristling in rage, I could imagine that a less seasoned warrior might have trembled in front of him. With a snarl he sprang at me with his sword, but whether he was a good swordsman or a poor one I never learned. With Dejah Thoris at my back I was no longer human—I was a superman, and no one could have stood against me!

With a single, low: "For the Princess of Helium!" I ran my blade straight through the rotten heart of Okar's rotten ruler. I then kicked him down the steps in front of the white, drawn faces of his nobles. Salensus Oll rolled to the floor at the foot of the steps below his marriage throne, dead as he could be.

For a moment, silence reigned in the room. Then the fifty nobles rushed me. We fought ferociously, but the advantage was mine. I stood up on a raised platform, and I fought for the most glorious woman on Barsoom, and I fought for a great love, and I fought for the mother of my boy.

From behind my shoulder, in the silvery cadence of her beautiful voice, rose the brave battle anthem of Helium that the nation's women sing as their men march out to victory. That alone was enough to inspire me to victory over those impossible odds, and I believe that I could have beaten the entire roomful of yellow warriors.

Fast and furious was the fighting as the nobles sprang, time and again, up the steps only to fall back bleeding and dying. They fought a swordsman that had gained a new wizardry from his experience with the cunning and skilled Solan.

Two were pressing me so closely that I could not turn when I heard a movement behind me and noted that the sound of the battle anthem had stopped. Was Dejah Thoris preparing to take her place beside me? Heroic daughter of a heroic world! It would be just like her to seize a sword and fight at my side.

But she did not come, and I was glad because it would have doubled my burden in protecting her. She must be contemplating some other cunning strategy, I thought, and so I carried on secure in the belief that my divine princess stood close behind me.

I must have fought there against the nobles for half an hour before even one placed a foot on the dais where I stood. Then, all of a sudden, they formed up below me for a last, mad, desperate charge. As they advanced, the door at the far end of the chamber swung open, and a messenger ran into the room.

"The Jeddak of Jeddaks!" he cried. "Where is the Jeddak of Jeddaks? The city has fallen to the enemy hordes, and now the main gate of the palace itself has been forced open! The warriors of the south are pouring into our sacred palace!

"Where is Salensus Oll? He alone will be able to revive the courage of our warriors. He alone will save the day for Okar. Where is Salensus Oll?"

The nobles stepped back from the dead body of their ruler, and one of them pointed to the corpse. The messenger staggered back in horror like he had received a blow in the face. He then shouted out, "Fly, nobles of Okar! Fly! Nothing can save you. Listen! Here they come!"

As he spoke, we heard the deep roar of angry men from the corridor, the clank of metal and the clang of swords. Without another glance at me, as I stood like a spectator watching the tragic scene, the nobles wheeled and fled the room.

Almost immediately a force of yellow warriors appeared in the doorway where the messenger had just entered. They were backing into the room, stubbornly resisting the advance of a handful of red men who forced them to slowly retreat.

Above the heads of the contestants, I could see the face of my old friend Kantos Kan. He was leading the party that had fought its way into the very heart of the palace.

In an instant I saw that by attacking the Okarians from the rear, I could disorganize them and that their further resistance would be short-lived. With me between Dejah Thoris and her enemies, and with Kantos Kan and his warriors attacking from the front, there could be no danger to Dejah Thoris standing there alone beside the throne.

I wanted the men of Helium to see me and

to know that their beloved princess was here, too. I knew that this knowledge would inspire them to even greater deeds of valor than they had performed thus far. As I crossed the room to attack the enemy from the rear, a small doorway at my left opened. To my surprise, I saw Matai Shang and his daughter, Phaidor, as they peered into the room.

They looked around quickly. Their eyes rested for a moment on the dead body of Salensus Oll, on the blood that covered the floor, on the corpses of the nobles who had fallen in front of the throne, and finally on me and the red warriors.

They did not enter the room, but scanned every corner from where they stood. After their eyes had covered the entire area, a look of fierce rage spread over the features of Matai Shang, while a cold and cunning smile touched the Phaidor's lips. Then they were gone, but not before a chilling laugh was thrown directly in my face by the woman.

At that time, I did not understand Matai Shang's rage or Phaidor's pleasure, but I knew that neither were good for me. A moment later I attacked the yellow men, and as the red men of Helium saw me a loud shout rang through the room and drowned out the noise of battle.

"For the Prince of Helium!" they cried. "For the Prince of Helium!" and, like hungry lions, they fell once more on the warriors of the North. The yellow men, cornered between two enemies, fought with desperation. They fought like I would fight if I had been in their place. They fought to take as many of their enemies with them as they could.

It was a glorious battle, but the end seemed inevitable. Suddenly, from down the corridor behind the red men, there appeared a large group of new, fresh yellow warriors. Now the tables were turned, and it was the men of Helium who seemed doomed to be ground between two mill-stones. Everyone was forced to turn and meet this new assault. I now had to continue the fight with the last of the nobles left inside the throne room.

They kept me so busy that I began to wonder if I would ever be finished with them. Slowly they pressed me back into the room, and when they had all gotten in after me, one of them closed and bolted the door. I was trapped without any hope of rescue from the outside.

It was a clever move: it put me at the mercy of a dozen men inside a locked room, and it cut off the escape of the red men in the outside corridor if their new enemies started to win this strange battle.

But I have faced worse odds, and I knew that Kantos Kan had battled his way out of more dangerous traps. So I knew I should just turn my attention to the business of the moment. My thoughts constantly went back to Dejah Thoris, and I longed for the moment when I could hold her in my arms and hear her words of love once again.

During the fighting in the chamber, I had not been able to steal a glance at her. I wondered why she was no longer singing the martial hymn of Helium; but I only needed the knowledge that I was battling for her safety to bring out the best in me.

It would be wearisome to tell the details of that bloody struggle; of how we fought from the doorway, the full length of the room to the very foot of the throne before the last of my antagonists fell with my blade in his heart.

I turned around to seize my princess and reap my reward for all the bloody encounters I went through for her sake from the South Pole to the North. The words died on my lips. My arms dropped to my sides like someone who suffered a mortal wound. I staggered up the steps to the throne. Dejah Thoris was gone!

CHAPTER
14

Rewards

Seeing that Dejah Thoris was not in the room made me remember the dark face looking through the drapes behind the throne when I interrupted the hateful wedding ceremony.

Why had I not been more careful? Once again Dejah Thoris was in the clutches of that archfiend, Thurid, the black dator of the First Born! All my labor was done for nothing! Now I realized the cause of Matai Shang's rage and Phaidor's face showing cruel pleasure.

They figured out what was happening, and the hekkador of the Holy Therns realized that Thurid had stolen Dejah Thoris. Phaidor's pleasure was because she knew what this would mean to me.

My first thought was to look behind the drapes at the back of the throne. I tore the priceless stuff from its fastenings and saw a narrow doorway. Was this Thurid's escape route? As I looked through the passageway, I spotted a tiny, jeweled ornament.

I snatched up the bauble and saw that it displayed the Princess of Helium's symbol! Holding it carefully, I dashed madly along the winding way as it led downward toward the lower galleries of the palace. I went only a short distance when I came to the room where I had left Solan. His dead body still lay on the floor, and there was no sign that anyone else had passed through the room, but I knew that Thurid and Dejah Thoris had gone this way.

For a moment I was uncertain as to which of the several exits from the room would lead me on the right path. I tried to remember the directions that I heard Thurid repeat to Solan, and at last Thurid's words came to me and I repeated them to myself.

"Go through that door, follow the corridor, passing three side corridors on the right; then go into the fourth right-hand corridor to where three corridors meet; take the one on the right, hugging the wall to avoid the pit trap. At the end go down a spiral runway; after that follow the tunnel to the exit."

I looked around the room and spotted the door he had pointed to as he spoke. I was off! I knew that there would be danger, but I threw caution to the wind! Part of the way was pitch black, but some was fairly well lighted. The stretch where I had to hug the wall to avoid the pit trap was darkest of them all. I was nearly over the edge of the pit before I knew that I was near the danger spot. A narrow ledge, maybe a foot wide, had been left to carry the knowledgeable around that deadly pit. But at last it was behind me, and then I saw a feeble light that made the rest of the way easy. At the end of the last corridor, I came out into the glare of day to see a field of snow and ice.

Leaving the warm temperature in the city of Kadabra, the sudden change to arctic frigidity was not pleasant. Almost naked, I knew I could not endure the bitter cold and would freeze to death before I could catch up with Thurid and Dejah Thoris.

To be blocked by nature seemed a cruel fate, and as I staggered back into the warmth, I was almost hopeless. I had not given up the pursuit, but if there were a safer way, the delay would be worth it. I wanted to come to Dejah Thoris in fit condition to do battle for her.

I had just returned to the tunnel when I stumbled over a fur garment that seemed fastened to the floor. In the darkness I could not see what held it, but I soon discovered that it was wedged beneath a closed door. Opening the door, I found a small chamber filled with the outdoor apparel of the yellow men. It was a dressing room used by the nobles leaving and entering the hothouse city. Thurid stopped here to outfit himself and Dejah Thoris before venturing into the bitter cold.

It took only a few seconds to put on the orluk-skin clothing along with the heavy, fur-lined boots. Once more I stepped outside to find the fresh tracks of Thurid and Dejah Thoris in the newly fallen snow. Now, at last, my task seemed easy, for though the going was rough, I knew the direction I should follow.

Through a snow-covered canyon, the trail led up toward the summit of low hills. Beyond these it dipped again into another canyon, only to rise a quarter-mile farther on toward a pass which skirted the flank of a rocky hill.

I could see by the signs on the trail that when Dejah Thoris had walked, she had been continually holding back, and that the black man had been forced to drag her. For other stretches, only his footprints were visible, deep and close together in the heavy snow, and I knew from these signs that he had to carry her. I could well imagine that she fought him every step of the way.

As I came around the hill's shoulder, I saw something that made my heart beat faster. Down in the valley four people stood in front of a cave. They were gathered around a flier that had just been dragged from its hiding place.

The four were Dejah Thoris, Phaidor, Thurid, and Matai Shang. The two men were engaged in a heated argument—the Father of Therns threatening, while the black scoffed at him. As I crept toward them, I saw that the men finally reached some sort of a compromise, for they both started dragging Dejah Thoris to the flier's deck.

They tied her up, and then they both went down to the ground again to fool around with some mechanical part of the aircraft. Phaidor entered the small cabin on the vessel's deck.

I had gotten within a quarter of a mile of them when Matai Shang spotted me. I saw him seize Thurid by the shoulder, wheeling him around in my direction as he pointed to where I was now plainly visible. I cast aside any attempt at stealth and broke into a mad race for the flier!

The two redoubled their efforts and had their tasks completed before I got close. Then they both made a rush for the boarding ladder. Thurid was the first to reach it and climbed to the boat's deck, where a touch of the button controlling the buoyancy tanks sent the craft slowly upward, though not with the speed that marks a well-conditioned flier.

I was still some hundred yards away as I saw them rising away from my grasp! Back at Kadabra was a fleet of fliers—the ships of Helium and

Ptarth that I had saved from destruction earlier in the day. But I knew that before I could reach them, Thurid would make good his escape.

As I ran, I saw Matai Shang clambering up the swaying, swinging ladder, while above him leaned the evil face of the First Born. A trailing rope from the vessel's stern gave me new hope— if I could reach it before it whipped too high I could use it to climb up to the deck.

Now Matai Shang was close to the gunwale. I watched as his hand was reaching up to grab the metal rail. Thurid leaned down toward his co-conspirator. Suddenly a raised dagger gleamed in the hand of the black. Down it drove toward the white face of the Father of Therns. With a loud shriek of fear, the Holy Hekkador tried to block that menacing arm.

I was almost to the trailing rope. The craft was still rising slowly and drifting away from me. Then I stumbled and fell, striking my head on a rock. I was only an arm's length from the end of the rope and watched as it left the ground.

I was stunned for only a few seconds while all that was dearest to me drifted farther from my reach in the clutches of that black fiend. When I opened my eyes, Thurid and Matai Shang were still fighting, and the flier drifted a hundred yards farther to the south. The end of the trailing rope was now a good thirty feet above the ground.

Goaded to madness when success was almost within my grasp, I tore frantically across the ice. Just beneath the rope's dangling end I put my earthly muscles to the supreme test. With a tremendous, catlike bound, I jumped upward toward that slender strand—the only means that could carry me to my vanishing love.

My fingers closed a foot above its lowest end. I felt the rope slipping, slipping through my grasp. I tried to raise my free hand to take a second hold above my first, but the change of position caused me to slip more rapidly toward the end of the rope.

Slowly I felt the tantalizing thing escaping me. In a moment, all that I had gained would be lost—then my fingers reached a knot at the very end of the rope!

With a prayer of gratitude, I scrambled upward toward the boat's deck. I could not see Thurid and Matai Shang now, but I heard the sounds of conflict and knew that they still fought. The Thern fought for his life and the black for the increased buoyancy that relief from the weight of even a single body would give the craft.

If Matai Shang died before I reached the deck, my chances of ever getting there would be slender indeed. The black dator would only need to cut the rope to be freed from me forever. As my hand clamped tight on the ship's rail, a horrid scream rang out below me that sent my blood cold. I turned my horrified eyes downward to see a shrieking, hurtling, twisting thing falling beneath me. It was Matai Shang, Holy Hekkador, Father of Therns, gone to his last accounting.

Then my head came above the deck, and I saw Thurid, dagger in hand, leaping toward me. He was at the forward end of the craft, while I was attempting to climb aboard near the vessel's stern. But only a few paces lay between us, and no power on Earth could get me up on that deck before he reached me.

I stopped trying to climb up over the gunwale. Instead, I took a firm grasp on the rail with my left hand and drew my dagger. I would at least die as I had lived—fighting.

As Thurid came opposite the cabin's doorway, a new element was added to the grim tragedy being enacted on the deck of Matai Shang's disabled flier. It was Phaidor. With flushed face, disheveled hair, and eyes that betrayed the recent presence of mortal tears, she leaped to the deck directly in front of me. In her hand was a long, slim dagger. I cast a last look at my beloved princess. Then I turned my face up toward Phaidor—waiting for the blow.

Never have I seen that beautiful face more beautiful than it was at that moment. It seemed incredible that one so lovely could harbor a heart so cruel and relentless. But today there was a new expression in her eyes that I had never seen before—an unfamiliar softness and a look of suffering.

Thurid was beside her now pushing past to reach me. What happened then occurred so quickly that it was all over before I realized it. Phaidor's slim hand shot out to grab his arm with the dagger. Her other hand went high with its gleaming blade. "That is for Matai Shang!" she cried, and she buried her blade deep in the dator's chest. "That is for the wrong you would have done Dejah Thoris!" and again the sharp steel sank into the bloody flesh.

"And that, and that, and that!" she shrieked, "For John Carter, Prince of Helium!" and with each word her sharp point pierced the vile heart of the villain. Then, with a shove, she rolled the carcass of the First Born under the guard rail to fall in awful silence after the body of his victim.

I had been paralyzed by surprise during the awe-inspiring scene, and I had made no move to reach the deck. I was still further amazed by her next act as Phaidor extended her hand and helped me up to the deck! I stood gazing at her and saw a wan smile touch her lips—it was not the cruel and haughty smile of the self-proclaimed goddess that I had seen before.

"You wonder, John Carter, what strange thing has caused this change in me? I will tell you. It is love—love for you," and when I darkened my brows in disapproval she raised an appealing hand.

"Wait," she said. "It is not my love for you—it is the love of Dejah Thoris for you that has taught me about true love. I now know that my selfish and jealous passion for you was far from real love.

"Now I am different. Now, perhaps, I could love someone like Dejah Thoris loves you. It would please me to know that you and she are once more united, for I know you have found true happiness with her.

"But I am unhappy because of the wickedness that I have caused. If Phaidor, daughter of the Holy Hekkador of the Holy Therns, has sinned, she has made partial reparation today. If you doubt my sincerity, I will prove it in the only way that lies open. I have saved you for someone else, so now Phaidor leaves you to her embraces."

With her last word, she turned and leaped from the vessel's deck into the abyss below. With a cry of horror, I sprang forward but was too late. I sadly turned away from the awful sight beneath the ship.

A moment later I cut Dejah Thoris loose, and as her arms went around my neck and her perfect lips touched mine, I forgot the horrors and suffering I had endured for so long.

CHAPTER
15

The New Ruler

Dejah Thoris and I checked out the craft and found it to be a completely useless flier. The buoyancy tanks leaked badly, and her engine would not even start. We were helpless and stuck there in mid air above the arctic ice.

The craft drifted across the chasm holding the corpses of Matai Shang, Thurid, and Phaidor, and now hung above a low hill. Opening the buoyancy escape valves, I lowered the ship slowly to the ground. As she landed, Dejah Thoris and I stepped from her deck and, hand in hand, turned back across the frozen waste toward the city of Kadabra.

We walked slowly for we had much to say to each other. She told me about that last terrible moment when the door of her prison cell inside the Temple of the Sun was slowly closing between us. She explained how Phaidor attacked her with a dagger, and that Thuvia's warning shriek saved her life.

It had been that cry that had rung in my ears all the long, weary months that I had been worrying about my beautiful wife's fate. Of course I had not known that Thuvia wrestled the blade away from the evil Thern before it hurt either Dejah Thoris or herself.

She told me, too, of the awful eternity of her imprisonment. She told me about the cruel hatred of Phaidor and the tender love of Thuvia, and how, even when despair was the darkest, they had clung to the same hope and belief—that John Carter would find a way to release them.

We entered the outside palace wall and soon came to Solan's chamber. We were walking without a care in the world since I was sure that by this time both the city and the palace would be in friendly hands. And so, tracing our way back, we barged into Solan's room into the midst of a dozen enemy warriors! They were escaping to the outside world along the corridors we had just traveled.

At sight of us they halted in their tracks, and then an ugly smile spread over the features of their leader. "The cause of all our misfortunes!" he cried, pointing at me. "We will have at least partial vengeance when we leave behind the corpses of the Prince and Princess of Helium.

"When they find these two," he went on, jerking his thumb upward toward the palace above, "they will realize that the vengeance of the yellow man costs his enemies dearly. Prepare to die, John Carter! Just to make your end more bitter, know that I may change my mind about giving a merciful death to your princess—perhaps she will be kept as a plaything for my men!"

I stood close to the instrument-covered wall—Dejah Thoris at my side. She looked up at me wonderingly as the warriors advanced with their drawn swords. Mine still hung in its scabbard at my side, but there was a smile on my lips.

The yellow warriors looked surprised as I made no move to draw my weapon. They hesitated, fearing a ruse; but their leader urged them on. When they had come almost within sword's reach I raised my hand and laid it on a certain lever, and then, still smiling grimly, I looked my enemies in the face.

They all came to a sudden stop, casting frightened glances at me and at one another. "Stop!" shrieked their leader. "You do not dream of what you do!"

"Right you are," I replied. "John Carter does not dream. He knows—knows that if one of you takes another step toward Dejah Thoris, Princess of Helium, I pull this lever, and she and I shall die together; but we shall not die alone."

The warriors stepped back, whispering together for a few moments. At last their leader turned to me. "Go on your way, John Carter," he said, "and we shall go ours."

"Prisoners do not go their own way," I answered, "and you are prisoners—prisoners of the Prince of Helium."

Before they could respond, a door opened, and a score of yellow men poured into the room. For an instant the warriors about to attack me looked relieved, but then they spotted the leader of the new party. Their faces fell as they recognized Talu, rebel Prince of Marentina and knew that they would find neither aid nor mercy at his hands.

"Well done, John Carter," he cried. "You turn their own mighty power against them. It is fortunate for Okar that you were here to prevent their escape, for these are the greatest villains north of the ice barrier. This one"—pointing to the leader of the party—"would have made himself Jeddak of Jeddaks. We would then have had an even more villainous ruler than the hated tyrant who fell before your sword."

The Okarian nobles now submitted to arrest, since nothing but death faced them if they tried to resist. Escorted by Talu's warriors, we made our way to the audience chamber where we found a vast assembly of warriors.

Red men from Helium and Ptarth, yellow men of the North, blacks of the First Born who had come under my friend Xodar, all came to help search for me and my princess. There were savage, green warriors from the dead sea bottoms of the south and even a handful of white-skinned Therns who had renounced their religion and sworn allegiance to Xodar.

There was Tardos Mors and Mors Kajak, and tall and mighty in his gorgeous warrior trappings, Carthoris, my son. These three ran to Dejah Thoris as we entered the apartment, and though the lives and training of royal Martians tend not toward emotional demonstration, I thought that they would suffocate her with their embraces.

And there was Tars Tarkas, Jeddak of Thark, and Kantos Kan, my old-time friends. Suddenly, leaping and tearing at my harness in the exuberance of his great love, was dear old Woola—mad with happiness.

Long and loud was the cheering that burst out at the sight of us! The din of ringing metal was deafening as the veteran warriors of every Martian nation and tribe clashed their blades together in token of success and victory! But as I passed among the throng of saluting nobles and warriors and jeds and jeddaks, my heart was heavy, for there were two faces missing. I would have given much to see Thuvan Dihn and

Thuvia, but they were not to be found in the chamber.

I made inquiries among men of every nation, and at last one of the yellow prisoners of war told me what happened. They were captured as they tried to reach me when I was in the Pit of Plenty. My informer said that they were now buried deep in the dungeons beneath the palace. They were to stay there until the tyrant of the North decided their fate.

A moment later search parties were scouring the ancient prison, and my cup of happiness was full when I saw them being escorted into the room by a cheering guard of honor.

Looking down on that crowded and happy chamber stood the silent and empty throne of Okar. Of all the strange scenes it must have witnessed since that long-dead age that had first seen a Jeddak of Jeddaks take his seat, none could compare with today. I pondered the past and future of that long-buried race of black-bearded yellow men. I thought that I saw a brighter and more useful existence for them among the great family of friendly nations that now stretched from the South Pole to their very doors.

It was twenty-two years ago that I had been cast, naked and a stranger, into this strange and savage world. At that time the hand of every race and nation was raised in continual strife and warring against the men of every other land and color. Today, by the might of my sword and the loyalty of my friends, black man and white, red man and green rubbed shoulders in peace and good fellowship.

All the nations of Barsoom were not yet together, but a great stride toward that goal had been taken. Now if I could entice the fierce yellow race into this solidarity of nations, I would feel that I had completed a great lifework. I would have repaid to Mars at least a portion of the immense debt of gratitude I owed her for giving me my Dejah Thoris.

And as I thought of this, I saw only one way and a single man who could insure the success of my hopes. As is ever the way with me, I acted then as I always act—without deliberation and without consultation. I grabbed Talu by the arm and dragged him up in front of the throne last occupied by Salensus Oll.

"Warriors of Barsoom," I cried, "Kadabra has fallen and with her the hateful tyrant of the North; but the integrity of Okar must be preserved. The red men are ruled by red jeddaks, the green warriors of the ancient seas acknowledge none but a green ruler, the First Born of the South Pole take their law from black Xodar! It would not be to the interests of either yellow or red man if a red jeddak were to sit on the throne of Okar.

"There is only one warrior best fitted for the ancient and mighty title of Jeddak of Jeddaks of the North. Men of Okar, raise your swords to your new ruler—Talu, the rebel Prince of Marentina!"

A great shout of rejoicing burst from the free men of Marentina and the Kadabran prisoners! They had all thought that the red men would keep what they had taken by force of arms, for such was the way on Barsoom. They had feared that they would be ruled by an alien Jeddak.

The victorious warriors, who had followed Carthoris, joined in the noisy demonstration. Amidst the wild confusion and tumult and cheering, Dejah Thoris and I went out into the garden of the jeddaks that graces the inner courtyard of the palace of Kadabra.

As we walked on a quiet and secluded path we spotted Thuvia of Ptarth and Carthoris of Helium sitting on a carved seat of wondrous beauty beneath a beautiful trellis of purple blooms. The handsome youth was bent above the beautiful face of his companion. I looked at Dejah Thoris, smiling, and as I drew her close I whispered: "Why not?"

Indeed, why not? What does age matter in this world of perpetual youth?

We remained at Kadabra, the guests of Talu,

until after his formal induction into office. At last we prepared to sail south across the ice barrier in the immense fleet which I had saved from destruction. Just as we formed up all the ships for a last flying salute circling Kadabra, we witnessed the total demolition of the grim Guardian of the North under orders of the new Jeddak of Jeddaks.

"From now on, the fleets of the red men and the black are free to come and go across the ice barrier just like in their own lands," he announced.

"The Carrion Caves will be cleaned so that the green men have an easy way into the land of the yellow men, and the hunting of the sacred apt shall be the sport of my nobles and guests until no single specimen of that hideous creature roams the frozen north."

We said farewell to our yellow friends with real regret and set sail for Ptarth. We stayed there for a month as the guest of Thuvan Dihn, and I could see that Carthoris would have remained there forever if he had not been a Prince of Helium.

We hovered above the immense forests of Kaol until word from Kulan Tith brought us to his single landing-tower. It took all day and half a night for our vessels to disembark their crews. At the city of Kaol we visited with the ruler and his high nobles, cementing the new ties that had been formed between Kaol and Helium. When we finally departed, we left many new friends behind.

Finally, on one long-to-be-remembered day, we sighted the tall, thin towers of the twin cities of Helium. The people had been preparing for our coming for a long time. The sky was gorgeous with brightly trimmed fliers. Every roof in both cities was spread with costly silks and tapestries.

Gold and jewels were scattered over roof and street and plaza, so that the two cities seemed ablaze with the fires of the hearts of the magnificent stones and burnished metal that reflected the brilliant sunlight, changing it into countless glorious hues.

At last, after twelve years, the royal family of Helium was reunited in their own city, surrounded by joy-mad millions dancing in front of the palace gates. Women and children and mighty warriors wept in gratitude for the fate that had restored their beloved Tardos Mors and the divine princess whom the whole nation idolized.

That night a messenger came to me as I sat with Dejah Thoris and Carthoris on the roof of my city palace. Years ago we had made a lovely garden where we could find seclusion and quiet happiness among ourselves, far from the pomp and ceremony of court. The message summoned us to the Temple of Reward—"where one is to be judged this night."

I racked my brain to think what important case there might be pending which could call the royal family from their palaces on the eve of their return to Helium after years of absence—but when the jeddak summons, no man delays.

As our flier touched the landing stage at the temple's top we saw countless other craft arriving and departing. In the streets below, thousands of citizens surged toward the gates of the temple.

Suddenly I remembered the deferred doom that awaited me since that time I had been tried here in the Temple by Zat Arras for the sin of returning from the Valley Dor and the Lost Sea of Korus.

Could it be possible that the strict sense of justice that dominates the men of Mars had caused them to overlook the great good that had come out of my heresy? Could they ignore the fact that to me, and me alone, was due the rescue of Carthoris, Dejah Thoris, Mors Kajak, and Tardos Mors?

I could not believe it, and yet why else could I have been summoned to the Temple of Reward immediately after the return of Tardos Mors to his throne?

My first surprise as I entered the temple and approached the Throne of Righteousness was to note the men who sat there as judges. There was Kulan Tith, Jeddak of Kaol, whom we had but

just left within his own palace a few days ago;
there was Thuvan Dihn, Jeddak of Ptarth—how
did he get to Helium so quickly?

There was Tars Tarkas, Jeddak of Thark, and
Xodar, Jeddak of the First Born; there was Talu,
Jeddak of Jeddaks of the North, whom I would
have sworn was still in his ice-bound hothouse
city beyond the northern barrier, and among
them sat Tardos Mors and Mors Kajak, with
enough lesser jeds and jeddaks to make up the
thirty-one who must sit in judgment upon their
fellow man.

A right royal tribunal indeed, and such a one,
I warrant, as never before sat together during all
the history of ancient Mars. As I entered, silence
fell upon the great concourse of people that
packed the auditorium.

Then Tardos Mors stood up. "John Carter,"
he said in his deep, martial voice, "take your place
upon the Pedestal of Truth, for you are to be
tried by a fair and impartial tribunal of your fellow men."

With level eye and high-held head I did as he
said, and as I glanced around that circle of faces
that a moment before I could have sworn contained the best friends I had on Barsoom, I saw
no single friendly glance—only stern, uncompro-
mising judges, there to do their duty.

A clerk holding a large book stood up and
read a long list of the more notable deeds that I

had to my credit. It covered the period of twenty-two years since I first stepped onto the sea bottom beside the incubator of the Tharks. He read all that I had done within the circle of the Otz Mountains where the Holy Therns and the First Born had held sway.

It is the way upon Barsoom to recite a man's virtues with his sins when he stands trial, and so I was not surprised that all that was to my credit should be read there to my judges. I was sure that they knew it all by heart—even down to the present moment.

When the reading had ceased Tardos Mors arose. "Most righteous judges," he exclaimed, "you have heard recited all that is known of John Carter, Prince of Helium—the good with the bad. What is your judgment?"

Then Tars Tarkas got slowly to his feet, unfolding all his mighty, towering height until he loomed, a green-bronze statue, far above us all. He turned a baleful eye upon me—he, Tars Tarkas, with whom I had fought through countless battles; whom I loved as a brother. I might have wept if I had not been so mad with rage that I almost whipped out my sword and attacked them all on the spot.

"Judges," he said, "there can be but one verdict. No longer may John Carter be Prince of Helium"—he paused—"but instead let him be called Jeddak of Jeddaks, Warlord of Barsoom!"

As the thirty-one judges sprang to their feet with drawn and upraised swords in unanimous agreement with the verdict, the storm broke throughout the length and breadth and height of that mighty building until I thought the roof would fall down from the thunder of the mad shouting.

Now, at last, I saw the grim humor of the method they had adopted to do me this great honor. The congratulations that I received first from the judges and then by the nobles erased my thoughts that there might be any hoax in the reality of the title they had given me.

After a few minutes, fifty of the most powerful nobles of the greatest courts of Mars marched down the broad Aisle of Hope carrying a splendid sedan chair on their shoulders. As the people saw who was being carried, the cheers that had previously rung out for me seemed insignificant. The sounds of cheering thundered through the vast edifice, for this was acclaim for Dejah Thoris, beloved Princess of Helium.

They carried her straight to the Throne of Righteousness, and Tardos Mors assisted her out of the chair and escorted her to my side. "Let the world's most beautiful woman share the honor of her husband," he said.

In front of them all I pulled my wife close and kissed her as the crowd went wild with joy.

Afterword

By the time *The Warlord of Mars* opens, a reader might forgive John Carter if he has almost forgotten that he was once an Earthling. So much has happened since Carter, a Civil War veteran and courtly Southern gentleman, was first transported from the hills of Arizona to the red planet that had always fascinated him. On Barsoom he has astonished everyone with his unmatchable Earth strength. He's mastered the language, become expert with the local weapons, learned to pilot the Barsoomian vehicles, tamed the savage Martian beasts, and bested all enemies. He has been proclaimed a prince of Helium and, most importantly, won the love and the hand of the dazzling Dejah Thoris, princess of Helium. The happy couple even have a son, the brave and noble Carthoris. Much of this story is told in the first book in the series, *A Princess of Mars*. In *The*

Gods of Mars, Carter's accomplishments grow even more impressive: he takes on an evil goddess, Issus, and rescues her followers from the clutches of a deadly false religion.

Naturally, all these triumphs could not occur without stepping on a few toes, and in *The Warlord of Mars,* John Carter is surrounded by jealous enemies on all sides. He is tormented by the beautiful but evil Phaidor, who would gladly kill Dejah Thoris in order to make John Carter her own husband. Thurid, who has been humiliated in a battle with John Carter, hates the Earthling and has sworn revenge on him. Matai Shang, the former leader of Issus' priestly clan, wants him dead as well. And seemingly all of Carter's enemies want Dejah Thoris, either to marry her or to humiliate her in order to make Carter suffer.

But fear not—John Carter has a knack for making the right friends. Fortunately for his continued survival, Carter is an unerring judge of character. If a person is trustworthy, Carter instantly knows it; if he is treacherous, Carter can tell that as well. Equally luckily, those who are good and decent also instantly take to Carter; on more than one occasion, we see a Barsoomian going against what seems to be his own self-interests simply because he wants to do Carter a good turn. Even animals, it seems, respond to Carter's superior qualities—Woola, the calot that Carter refers to as his "faithful hound," belongs to a breed of previously savage, untamable beasts.

Considering Carter's amazing good fortune, you might think that the *Mars* series would lack suspense. After all, the more of the Mars stories you read, the more confident you become that Carter is going to triumph over any adversity. But somehow, author Burroughs keeps our attention. No matter what awful, death-defying scrape Carter has just been through, Burroughs comes up with an even more unlikely one next. At the end of almost every chapter, we're left thinking, "How the heck is he going to get out of this?" In that way, John Carter might remind you of other popular heroes of books and movies, such as Burroughs' own creation *Tarzan of the Apes*, or Hollywood's James Bond or Indiana Jones. All of them appeal to our endless taste for adventure, escapism, and excitement—even (or maybe especially!) when their adventures are a little on the unrealistic side. John Carter's adventures have kept readers on the edges of their seat for nearly a century. Like the natives of Barsoom, we can't get enough of this gallant Earth warrior.